MW00697970

BROKEN PROMISE

JULIA CRANE
TALIA JAGER

Broken Promise: A Between Worlds Novel
Copyright © 2012 Julia Crane and Talia Jager
Published by Valknut Press, LLC

ISBN: 978-1-62411-039-9
ISBN: 1-62411-039-8
Print edition
All rights reserved.

This book is protected under the copyright laws of the United States of America. Any reproduction or other unauthorized use of the material or artwork herein is prohibited. No part of this book may be used or reproduced in any manner whatsoever without prior written permission of the author.

This novel is a work of fiction. Any references to historical events; to real people, living or dead; or to real locales are intended only to give the fiction a sense of reality and authenticity. Names, characters, places, and incidents either are the product of the author's imagination or are used fictitiously, and their resemblance, if any, to real-life counterparts is entirely coincidental.

Cover Art by Eden Crane Design
Editing by Christine LePorte
Formatted by Eden Crane Design

Dedication

To our beta readers. Your insight is invaluable.

CHAPTER ONE

As I belted out the last note of my solo, my eyes caught a flicker of teal in the back of the auditorium. The sighting was brief and happened so fast I almost missed it through the harsh glare of the stage lights. Even lost in the music and half-blind, I would have known those wings anywhere.

Kallan.

My heart sped up, atnd my palms grew clammy. I searched the back of the auditorium, though I had the presence of mind to keep the note strong. Could he really be here? And if so...why?

Thunderous applause erupted as soon as the music trailed off into silence. Mrs. Lopez's amplified voice said brightly, "Rylie McCallister, ladies and gentleman! Isn't her voice just lovely?"

I barely noted her praise as I smiled and bowed. Gathering up the hem of my long, black evening dress, I rushed off the stage, taking the stairs at a quick yet cautious trot. The last thing I needed was to trip in front of everyone. I ignored the gawking stares of my fellow choir members and my family in the front row; I'd barely given them a chance to cheer for me.

I hurried up the aisle, my eyes still frantically searching the darkened hallway in the back of the auditorium for Kallan. He was just there; he couldn't have gone far. The applause continued, as if my abrupt exit was some strange part of the show. At the top of the ramp, I hit the doors, shoving on the bar to open them, and spilled into the lobby.

A quick look left and right verified what I'd already expected: My search was in vain. He wasn't there. The lobby was empty of anyone but a gray-haired man in a blue janitor's uniform collecting trash.

My heart sank. Maybe I had imagined it.

I touched the necklace of black stones that encircled my neck. It was an ever-present reminder of Kallan, the dark faery who had somehow kept a part of my heart when I left him. It had been a year since I last saw him, and I still had a year until I was supposed to return to him and the dark faery world. The only reason I'd even agreed to such a thing was that my family had been threatened. I clenched my fist tightly to my side at the thought of Varwik, Kallan's father and the leader of the dark faeries.

Despite the hatred I felt for Varwik, there was a deep-seated part of me that yearned to see Kallan again. I shook my head and tried to push away the sadness that had washed over me.

"Hey, beautiful."

Startled, I spun around and came face-to-face with Adam, my long-time boyfriend. His shaggy brown hair fell over his forehead above sparkling green eyes as he beamed at me.

"Oh. Hi." I could hear the detachment in my voice,

but I was too bothered by the thought of Kallan to even care.

"Are you okay?"

I cringed inwardly as I realized what my flight from the auditorium probably looked like to the people who loved me. "I'm fine."

"What are you doing out here?"

"I thought I saw someone." Damn the not-being-able-to-lie thing. There were some aspects of being a faery that were cool. The inability to lie, not so much.

Adam looked around and then back down at me. "Who?"

I hesitated. Adam didn't know about my time imprisoned in the dark faery world, and I wasn't going to share now, either. He certainly didn't know I had feelings for another guy. "Just someone I haven't seen in a while."

As usual, Adam took my explanation at face value and didn't press further.

"You were awesome! Like always," he said, the pride evident on his face. He ran his warm hand up my bare shoulder, sending shivers down my spine. What was I doing thinking about Kallan when I had the perfect boyfriend in front of me?

I blushed. "Thanks."

"Let's get back inside. Your parents were worried when you rushed out."

With one last look behind me, I followed him through the heavy metal doors. The choir was wrapping up the last song of the evening. I should have been up there with them, and I would probably get a lecture from Mrs. Lopez about it, but I didn't care. I sank into the empty seat next to my mom and willed myself not to turn around in search of Kallan.

"Are you okay?" my mother whispered.

"Fine," I mumbled. I wasn't about to get her worked up. My parents had done their best over the last year to try to act like none of this had happened, that I was just a normal girl instead of a faery with strong powers. They always told me if I wanted to talk about it they were there for me, but I didn't want to talk about it. I tried to convince myself that it was all a terrible mistake or some kind of dream that I would eventually wake up from. Although the wings sticking out of my back were good proof that wasn't going to happen.

And the necklace was verification that Kallan really did exist. Not to mention my faery mother, who was desperately trying to be a part of my life. I knew it was time to let her in, but I just couldn't. At least not yet. I had to give her credit, though; she was being very patient.

The audience clapped again at the end of the last song. The curtains closed, and I felt my mother's eyes on me. I turned to her and bit down on my lip, ready for whatever scolding was about to take place.

"What happened? Why did you run off?" she asked.

"I'll tell you when I get home," I said in a hushed voice. I didn't like to talk about anything related to faeries where other people could overhear. It was still hard enough for me to believe it, much less letting some stranger in on the secret.

My mother's eyes widened in surprise, but she quickly composed herself. "You better go talk to your teacher."

I knew she was right, but I didn't want to. "I'll meet you at home?"

"Is Adam going to bring you?"

"Yeah."

"Okay."

We all stood up and collected our belongings. As I turned to leave, my mother's soft voice rang out. "Rylie?"

"Yeah?"

"You sang beautifully."

I felt the heat rise to my cheeks. "Thanks."

I slipped my hand into Adam's, and we walked through the dark, silent halls of school to the choir room. When the big wooden door loomed in front of me, I let out a heavy sigh.

He pulled me to him without a word and kissed me with his soft lips. I closed my eyes and returned the embrace, letting myself forget my worries for the moment. When we broke apart, he said, "Don't worry. You were so good out there, she can't be mad at you."

"I hope you're right." I swept his light brown bangs out of his eyes. "I'll be right out."

"Good luck."

I took a deep breath and opened the door. The rest of the choir was already in the room, seated in their usual chairs around the U-shaped bleachers. Everyone turned to look at me. I ignored them, smiling at Mrs. Lopez as I walked up to her. "I'm sorry I rushed out of there like that."

She turned her back on the class, her concerned voice low as she asked, "Are you sick, Rylie?"

"No."

She looked at me, probably trying to figure out what had happened. "I assume it was something important."

I didn't answer with words, but I nodded. It was important to me, finding out if I'd seen Kallan. What my music teacher considered important, however, was up for debate.

"Don't let it happen again."

"I won't."

She turned back to the rest of the class. "Very well done, class. I'm so proud of you! All your hard work has paid off, so now go enjoy your weekend. I'll see you Monday."

I went back out to the hallway where Adam stood. It felt so good having someone there waiting for me. "She didn't yell."

"Told ya."

As he hugged me, I noticed another flash of teal from my peripheral vision. I stiffened, my gaze snapping towards it in time to see the girls' bathroom door inch shut.

What in the world?

My heart fluttering, I stepped back from Adam's arms and motioned to the bathroom. "Gimme a minute."

He rolled his eyes. "Girls."

I laughed at the face he made, and then cautiously pushed open the bathroom door.

At first glance, it was empty. Fluorescent lights made the tile walls bright and shiny. The left wall was lined with mirrors and reflected the cream-colored stalls.

I pushed open every stall, and then checked the dark corner beneath the window. There was no one inside. And frankly, why would Kallan have gone into a girls' bathroom anyway? I was so paranoid I was seeing things. That had to be it.

When I stopped in front of one of the mirrors, I could see a reflection of the real me in the mirror. The faery me.

My wings fluttered behind me a few times. They were shaped like a butterfly's and were a shimmering mixture of pink, lavender, and white. I liked my wings; I'd only just gotten used to them being there. I think the thing that bothered me the most were my pointy ears. I could definitely deal with the flawless skin and not needing to wear makeup anymore, but the ears annoyed me.

There was also the star-shaped birthmark on my face—the one that refused to be covered up —that marked me as an Aurorian faery. A rare breed with powers that far surpassed anyone in the faery world.

A responsibility I really didn't want.

The door opened. I quickly turned on the water, pretending like I was washing up.

A girl from choir walked in and stood next to me, fixing the clip in her curly brown hair. "Hey, Rylie."

"Hi, Lara." Looking between her and myself in the mirror felt awkward. She was a normal-looking human, and I was a faery with pointed ears and wings. She couldn't see my true form, though. Humans couldn't see past the glamour that made me look normal. I smiled at her. "See ya later."

I waved as I left the bathroom, glancing at the stalls again and hoping for a glimpse of teal wings.

Back out in the hallway, Adam put his arm around me as we started walking. "So what are we going to do tomorrow night?"

"I don't care. What did you have in mind?"

"Movie? Dinner? Whatever. As long as I'm with you, I'm happy."

I laid my head against his shoulder, silently berating myself for being so crazy over an imagined glimpse of Kallan. Who cared? Adam was my everything. "A movie sounds good."

The doors clicked shut behind us as we exited the side entrance into the brisk evening. From the front of the building, I heard the sound of the auditorium emptying, and a steady line of red taillights stretched towards the road. Adam's silver pickup truck waited in the parking lot, alone but for a few of my class-mates' cars.

Adam opened my door for me and then got in on the driver's side. He started the truck as he said, "I have baseball practice at ten, so I'll text you."

"Okay." I looked out the window and watched the streetlights pass. Adam turned on the radio, but kept the volume low.

I didn't realize I'd been searching the darkness until Adam killed the engine in my driveway. My eyes darted to the tree line, looking for a sign that Kallan was here.

"You seem a little distracted," Adam said.

"Sorry."

"You sure everything is okay?"

"Mhmm." It wasn't okay; I was obsessed with Kallan. But I couldn't tell my boyfriend that. I scooted closer to him and looked from his green eyes to his lips.

He took that as the invitation it was, and our lips met. I put my hand on the back of his head, deepening the kiss as I pressed my body against his. A minute later, we broke apart, breathless.

"Thanks for coming tonight," I murmured, smoothing my hands over his shirt.

"I wouldn't have missed it for anything. You know that."

I nodded. It was true. He'd never been anything but supportive. "See you tomorrow."

I couldn't help but scan the forest one more time as I took the sidewalk to the house. When my faery mother had initially sought me out to warn me that my sixteenth birthday would bring some major changes—wings and pointy ears—she used to hide out in the trees and watch me. If Kallan was in my world, he could be doing the same thing.

Exhaustion hit me as I entered the house through the garage door. My parents waited at the kitchen table, and they didn't look very happy.

Great.

"Spill," my mother said sternly.

I shrugged out of my light jacket and hung it on the rack next to the door. "I thought I saw someone."

"So you rushed off stage?" Dad asked. He was using his "detective voice," the one generally reserved for criminal investigations.

"Yes."

"Who did you think you saw?" my mother asked.

"Kallan."

Her light brown eyes showed a hint of recognition at the mention of his name. "The faery boy who helped you get home last year?"

"Yes." And the one who I'm promised to marry. The one I dream about a few times a week. The one my heart aches for...no matter how hard I try to forget him.

"Did you talk to him?" my father asked with his arms across his chest.

"Nope. He wasn't there."

"What do you mean 'he wasn't there'?" Dad barked. He hated not getting straight answers. "You didn't see him or you thought you saw him?"

"Didn't you say faeries can disappear at will?" my mother asked. I knew they constantly worried that I would get abducted again. The tension between her eyebrows proved that was foremost on her mind.

"I honestly don't know if I saw him or just imagined it," I said irritably.

My mom was right. I'd briefly forgotten that faeries could disappear at will, which meant I probably had seen Kallan. The thought both terrified and excited me more than I wanted to admit.

CHAPTER TWO

The next morning, I stood at my bedroom window and gazed out at darkening clouds that promised a storm. I often found myself rooted to this spot in the hope I'd catch a glimpse of Kallan. The edge of the woods that lined our property was the last place I'd seen him, almost a year ago. His pained expression was still etched in my mind.

I couldn't help but wonder if he was really back or if I had imagined the whole thing. So much time had passed. I figured he'd moved on and forgotten me. I constantly caught myself wondering what he was doing, who he was with, or if he thought about me.

I closed the curtain and scolded myself for acting so ridiculous. It should have been Adam that I thought of so much. He was the one I loved.

The hardest part of all was I had nobody to talk to about my dilemma. The only people that knew about Kallan were my parents, and there was no way I could tell them about my conflicting feelings for him. They wouldn't understand. They saw him as the enemy.

I pushed Kallan out of my mind and started getting ready. My best friend, Sierra, would be over to pick me up soon.

After my shower, I stepped into a blue shirt with a low back to complement my eyes. One of the most annoying things about being a faery had been finding clothes that my wings felt comfortable in. It was a lot harder than one would think. Sometimes I had to suck it up and wear clothes that weren't comfortable.

Since I no longer had to bother with makeup, I pulled my long blonde hair in a quick ponytail and ran down the stairs.

My dad was standing behind the counter in the kitchen reaching for a coffee mug. "Morning, Rylie."

"You're just getting up?" I peeked at the clock. It was ten o'clock, and he was still in his pajamas. My father was a morning person, so sleeping late was totally out of character. He looked even more ridiculous with his dark hair sticking up all over the place.

"My case load has kept me up late this month. I figured I'd sleep in and take it easy today," Dad answered with a twinkle in his eyes. Considering I'd dropped a bomb on them last night about seeing Kallan, he was in good spirits.

I glanced over at my mom and raised an eyebrow. Mom, who was still dressed in her plaid pajamas and had her chestnut hair up in a messy bun, just smiled and shrugged. Well, good for them, I thought. They deserved some relaxing time.

I grabbed the orange juice from the fridge and poured a glass.

Mom spoke up. "I got your favorite banana nut bread from Smith's. It's in the breadbox."

Finally, after years of trying to bake, my mom was

starting to accept some things were better to purchase than make herself. She meant well, but cooking was not her strong suit.

"Where are you off to this early?" she asked.

I pulled the loaf out of its bag and set it on the cutting board. "Figured I'd go out with Sierra for the day. She's having a hard time at home with her nephew being there and her mom and sister fighting. I thought it would be good for her if she got out of the house."

Mom took a sip of her coffee before she asked, "Why wasn't she at your concert? I don't think she's ever missed one before."

"She had to babysit again." I cut off a thick slice of the moist bread and took a bite.

"She's been doing that a lot lately. It doesn't really seem fair. I'm surprised her mother is allowing it."

"I know." I sighed. My best friend and I hadn't had a lot of time together lately, and I missed her. I really wanted to talk to her and tell her everything that had happened last year, but I was afraid she'd laugh or think I was crazy—or even be scared of me. That would crush me. I couldn't stand the thought of losing my best friend.

"Well, if nothing else I'm sure it's good birth control for her." My dad smirked. "Maybe you should offer to babysit."

"Funny." I rolled my eyes. Why did dads have to be such dorks?

I chugged my orange juice and had just put the glass in the dishwasher when Sierra's horn blared from out front. "I'm meeting Adam later."

"Okay. Have fun," Mom chirped.

"I'll be home by curfew." I shoved the last bite of bread in my mouth and grabbed my purse off the chair.

"Careful. It looks like a storm is coming," my father warned.

"We'll probably just go to the mall." With a quick wave, I slipped through the door and closed it behind me.

Sierra's black convertible sat on the street. The wind almost blew me off my feet as I trotted down the driveway, which explained why she didn't have the top down.

I slid into the passenger seat and scanned my best friend. She had dark circles under her green eyes, and the blonde highlights in her brown hair had faded. Sierra was always pulled together. I didn't quite know what to make of her appearance.

"Rough night?" I asked.

"You have no idea. That kid wakes up like every hour and my sister sleeps through half of it. I can't stand for the poor little guy to be crying, so I drag myself out of bed. I feel like a zombie."

"Not to be mean, but you kinda look like one, too."

She swatted me, and then pulled away from the curb.

"So where are we going?"

"I don't know. Want to catch a movie or hang out at the mall?" she asked. "As long as there are no babies involved, I'm all for it."

I laughed. "No babies. Got it. Maybe we could just hang out, do a little retail therapy, and talk."

Sierra smiled. "Sounds perfect. You meeting Adam later?"

"Yeah. He's supposed to text me."

We spent the next couple hours walking through the mall, stopping at various stores and spending money. Sierra had two credit cards to her name and used them constantly. I was actually worried for her. I wasn't sure what would happen to her when she graduated and didn't have her parents to spoil her.

We stopped in the food court and picked up cookies and sodas, then sat down at a table. As we unwrapped our goodies, I said, "Sierra?"

"Yeah?" She shoved a bite in her mouth.

"Do you think it would be cool to have some kind of power?"

"Like a superhero power?" She wiped crumbs off her mouth with the back of her hand.

"Sure. Something like that," I agreed, tearing off a gooey chunk of chocolate chip cookie.

"Yeah. Why not? I've always thought it would be awesome if I could read minds."

"A mind reader?" I wrinkled my nose. "Why would you want that power?"

Sierra shrugged. "It would be cool to know what others were thinking. You could use it to your advantage."

"What about looking different? Would you be okay if you looked differently than others? In order to have a power, I mean."

She shot me a weird look. "What would be different about me?"

"I dunno. Weird hair color or an extra-large nose or maybe wings?"

"Is this about your birthmark again?"

I thought about that for a second. "In a way."

She shook her head. "I think your birthmark is cool."

You wouldn't if it marked you the way it does me, I thought. "Just answer the question."

"I guess if I had something different about me, I'd have to live with it. Not sure I'd like a big nose. I could work with different color hair. Wings would be...

interesting."

I laughed. That was true. They were interesting. "Do you think there are creatures out there that we don't know about?"

"Sure. You know I think anything is possible." She smiled around a mouthful of cookie crumbs.

"What would you do if you found out they were walking around right beside us?"

She laughed. "As long as they're not biting me, I'm okay with that."

It was my turn to roll my eyes. "Not just vampires. Not all fantasy creatures are vampires."

"True. I think my opinion stays the same though. As long as they're not hurting me, I don't care."

Maybe it was time to tell her? She'd always had an open mind. I really thought she would be cool with it. For the next ten minutes, I tried to tell her a dozen different ways, but the words just wouldn't come out. I kept chickening out, and then finally decided to wait for another day.

My phone dinged. I took it out of my pocket and checked it. It was Adam.

4 good for u?

Yes. Already at mall. Meet here?

Ok. Food court.

Checking the time, I told Sierra, "Adam will be here in half an hour."

"Guess girl time is over."

"How are things with Ian?" I asked. Sierra and Ian had been dating since last spring, but lately they had seemed to be slipping apart. Of course I hadn't been around her much to know what the story was there.

She shrugged. "Complicated."

"Aren't all relationships?"

Sierra rolled her eyes. "What would you know

about relationship issues? You have the perfect boy-friend."

I was lucky to have Adam, and I knew it. I just wished I could shake the thought of a certain dark faery. Not to mention the fact that I was promised to said dark faery and would have to crush Adam to keep that promise. My stomach tied itself into knots just thinking about it.

We made another loop around the mall, and then parted ways. I met Adam in the food court with a kiss and a smile.

"Have you been at the mall all day?" he asked.

"Yup, since about ten-thirty."

"I'll never understand girls and shopping."

"It's our bonding time. Sierra needed to get out." I threw my arm around Adam's waist, and we made our way to the theater.

We decided on a comedy, where we laughed a lot and ate too much popcorn. I found myself glancing at Adam during the movie. His laugh was infectious and his smile could light up a room. There was no way I could give him up. I needed to find a way out of this crazy deal I'd made with Varwik. He was expecting me to move to the faery world and take my place beside Kallan when I turned eighteen. My feelings for Kallan were stressful and confusing, but I knew I cared for Adam. I didn't want to give him—or the rest of my life—up.

The rain had started while we were inside the theater. I shivered and Adam pulled me in close. The warmth of his body spread to mine as we hurried to the truck. Even though it was spring, a chill lingered in the air, especially when it was raining.

"Food or home?" he asked after we were settled in the cab.

"Ugh, I'm so full from the popcorn, but you know, a shake sounds good," I responded, thinking how ridiculous it sounded that I was cold and wanted a shake.

He drove to our favorite eating place, Bob's Diner. It was a cottage-style restaurant off the beaten path with pretty red shingles and a plaster hamburger out front. We both loved pretty much everything on the menu.

Come to think of it, Adam and I shared a lot of interests. We both liked movies, junk food, and music. He had always been supportive of my singing, and I encouraged his baseball.

We fit together perfectly, and I was scared that Varwik would tear us apart.

The wind cut off as soon as the door slammed shut behind us. A waitress nodded from behind the soda counter, and motioned for us to have a seat.

Our usual booth was right near the door, but the place was just busy enough that the wind would be too strong and cold coming inside, so we took a booth near the back.

The waitress came to take our order, her pen poised over her pad. "What'll it be, kids?"

"Can we have an order of..." I started.

"Fries," Adam finished. "And two chocolate milk-shakes."

I laughed and took his hand as she walked away. We sat silently for a moment as Adam spun the charm bracelet around on my arm. He had given it to me for my sixteenth birthday with two initial charms on it: a musical note and a heart. Then for Christmas, he gave me a butterfly and a snowflake.

"Do you want more charms for your birthday?" Adam asked.

My seventeenth birthday was a few weeks away and anything from him was special. I nodded. "You know I love them."

"I guess this was a good present, then."

"It was one of the best," I responded honestly, but there was a plaintive note in my voice that even I could hear. Adam always knew what I liked. I used to say he knew everything about me, but that wasn't true anymore.

His thumb brushed over the back of my hand. "What's wrong?"

"I just worry about losing you."

Surprised, he said, "Why would you worry about that?"

I looked away, out into the dim evening where the rain continued to pour. I don't know why, but things felt like they were coming to a head. It wasn't just the fact that I'd seen what I thought was Kallan not once, but twice, or that I felt eyes on me when there were none. There was something else at work.

I finally caught Adam's eye and murmured, "Something could come in between us."

"That won't happen," he said firmly, squeezing my hands. "I love you, Rylie."

"I love you, too," I responded, forcing a smile as the waitress returned with our shakes.

I knew I was in trouble when I got home and found my parents sitting at the table. It was never good when I found them waiting for me there. Frown lines had taken over Dad's forehead, and Mom was rubbing her temples.

Swallowing hard, I sat down. "What's going on?"

Mom slid over a piece of paper. "This."

I glanced down. My progress report. I scanned it quickly. My normal A's and B's had been replaced with C's and D's. There was a teacher comment that read "In danger of failing."

"Do you have an explanation, young lady?" Dad asked sternly.

I sagged against my seat. It wasn't like I hadn't seen it coming. I'd noticed the steady decline in my grades. "Not really."

Dad frowned. "Rylie."

"It's just hard, Dad," I said, rubbing my face. "It's hard being what I am and dealing with school. I don't know. I've just been struggling a lot more lately."

"We understand you are going through a lot, but this is not acceptable. There are only a couple months of school left. You want to be able to choose your college, don't you?"

I crossed my arms. "Have you forgotten I might not even get a chance to go to college? If Varwik has his way, I'll be the wife of a dark faery."

My father shook his head. "That's not going to happen."

"No one has found me a way out of this mess. I'm sorry if that seems a little more important." I paused. The clock on the wall ticked into the silence. "Don't worry. I'll bring my grades up."

"Honey, I really think you need to let Azura help you. She might be able to come up with a solution to get you out of the promise." My mother's eyes had softened. I knew it wasn't easy for her to tell me to ask Azura for help. Azura was my biological mother, something my mom could never truly be. But to me, Azura was a stranger—one that had completely ruined my life.

"I'll think about it." I stood up, ignoring my mom as she said my name, and plodded up the stairs. I slammed my door and threw myself onto the bed.

As if I didn't have enough to worry about, now they were harping on my grades.

CHAPTER THREE

The next day, Sierra and I went to the spring carnival being held at the local fairgrounds. It was an annual thing the town did every year around the first day of spring, and I always went with my best friend. She almost had the baby, but luckily she managed to talk her mom into watching him.

We went on rides and played games for a couple hours, then sat down for a treat. As I bit into my cotton candy, something caught my attention. Something fluttering in the meadow behind us. I froze, and then slowly turned to look.

Wings. Teal and black wings. My body went cold. Kallan looked right at me, his face still, but his wings moving. My wings did the same.

It was definitely him. The same slick black hair and penetrating blue-green eyes, a guy so gorgeous he couldn't be real...and he was standing only a few feet away. I felt like I was going to hyperventilate.

"Rylie?" Sierra ducked her head to catch my eye.

"Rylie? Are you okay? You look like you've seen a ghost."

I tore my gaze from Kallan. "What?"

"What's wrong?"

"Nothing. I...I..." I stammered. I glanced back towards Kallan, but he was gone. I stood up and spun around, searching for him, but there was no sign of him. Either he'd left or he'd gone invisible.

But he'd wanted me to see him.

Why was he here? He hated the human world. He'd told me that his mother had been killed here. I wasn't supposed to return to him until I was eighteen, and that was still a year away. Maybe he knew I was trying to get out of the whole thing and was here to make sure I didn't. The thought sent a chill of fear through me.

"Rylie, what are you looking for?" Sierra broke through my inner turmoil again. "I wish you'd talk to me."

Giving up on my search, I sat back down and stared at my cotton candy. It suddenly seemed tasteless. "About what?"

Sierra pursed her lips and looked to the side, like she was trying to think of what to say. "You've been different. Something's up with you, and you won't tell me what's going on."

Here it was. My big chance to tell her. Would I chicken out again? I ran through some lines in my head, trying to figure out the best way to say what I needed to. Nothing sounded good. "There is something going on. It's big and I'm..."

"You're what?"

"Scared."

She looked perplexed. "Of?"

"Losing you. Losing Adam."

"It must be huge if you're worried about losing us. What did you do?"

"I didn't 'do' anything. It's who I am."

She reached over and took my hand. "You're my best friend."

"I hope so."

"Rylie!" She sounded offended.

"It's going to sound crazy." I glanced around. We were on the outskirts of the fair, so we weren't really close enough to the crowd to be overheard.

She turned and looked at me expectantly, and then her eyes widened. "You're not pregnant, are you?"

"What? No! You have to have sex for that to happen."

Sierra laughed. "Whew, you scared me for a moment."

I let out a long breath. I just had to spit it out, no hesitations. "I'm a faery."

She was quiet for a minute. "Um...what?"

"A faery. Wings. Magick."

My best friend burst out laughing. "You really had me there for a minute."

Crap, she thought I was kidding. I sat down on the bench beside her. "Sierra, this isn't a joke. I'm not human. I'm a faery."

She stopped laughing and looked at me. "You look so serious."

"I am. It's the truth."

"You're telling me you're a faery...like Tinkerbell? Aren't faeries supposed to be like an inch tall? You can't be serious, Ry—"

She reminded me of myself just a year ago. "No. Those are piskies," I corrected her. Now I sounded like Azura.

"Of course they are," Sierra retorted sarcastically.

"And isn't it *pixies?*"

"Apparently not."

She raised an eyebrow. "What's going on, Rylie?"

"On my sixteenth birthday, I found out I was a faery."

"A faery?" she repeated.

"This lady showed up claiming to be my birth mother. She told my parents their baby died, and she had switched babies because she had to keep me safe."

Sierra stared at me. "What?"

"This woman then told us I wasn't human. We didn't really believe her until she showed us her wings."

"Wings?"

I nodded, thinking maybe my best friend was in shock by the way she kept repeating everything I said.

"So that means you have wings?" Sierra peered around my back. "I don't see wings."

"They're hidden."

Sierra raised an eyebrow. "Under your shirt?"

I laughed. "No, they're quite big."

I could tell she wasn't going to believe me until I proved it to her. I looked around. There were a couple of people within sight, and I couldn't risk them seeing me. I motioned for her to stand up. "Follow me."

We passed back through all the games and weaved in and out of the crowds as my eyes scanned the carnival for somewhere to go. I spotted a large shed behind the petting zoo and dragged her towards it.

I peeked inside to see if anyone was there, but it appeared to be abandoned; no tools or equipment at all. I looked around to make sure nobody was watching, and then stepped inside, quickly shutting the door behind us. I turned to face Sierra. "Ready?"

She nodded, staring at me like I'd lost my mind. Quickly, before I could lose my nerve, I dropped my glamour.

Her eyes widened in shock. She circled around me. I felt her touch my wings, and the usual tingle of sensation filled me. Then she tugged. I guess she wanted to see if they came off and this would all be a joke.

Although I stayed silent and let her absorb the situation, I really wanted to know how she felt. Would she still want to be my friend? Would she freak out and run away? Or would she go tell Adam?

After what seemed like a lifetime, she finally she broke the silence. "This is surreal."

"Tell me about it." I was getting a little self-conscious being in my true form, so I glamoured myself again.

"What did you just do?" Sierra waved her hands around behind by back.

"I made myself look human again."

"How?"

"Something called glamour."

Sierra leaned against the wall, her arms crossed over her chest. "So. You're a faery."

"Yes."

"And your biological mom gave you away."

"Yes."

"Because she needed to keep you safe?"

"Right."

"Why?"

"Apparently my father wanted to trade me for some dark magick."

"Nice guy," Sierra said wryly.

I examined her, trying to find any sign that she was about to freak out. But she didn't seem to be nervous or anything. "So...you're okay with this?" I asked.

Sierra wrinkled her nose, and then grinned. "It's a little weird, but yeah."

I rejoiced inside, thrilled that she wasn't freaking out. If I shared everything with her—the kidnapping, my time in captivity, all of it, then I would finally have someone to talk to when things got rough.

"So what had you so freaked out back there? Something to do with this faery thing, right?"

"I saw another faery." I walked to the window and peeked out. There was no sign of Kallan. Detached from the sighting of him, I started to question if I hadn't imagined him. I was so stressed out lately that it was a possibility.

"Why does another faery freak you out?"

"Long story. Basically there's this faery boy I'm supposed to marry."

"What?" Sierra gasped.

"Yeah. That's obviously a problem."

"And he was here?"

"Yes, but he's gone now."

Sierra lowered her voice, as if she didn't really want to ask. "Does Adam know?"

"NO!" I responded quickly. "Please don't tell him. Don't tell anyone."

"I doubt anyone would believe me."

"I'm serious."

"I am, too!" She shook her head. "So, you're supposed to marry some faery?"

I nodded.

"When?"

"When I'm eighteen. I need to find a way to get out of it."

Sierra looked at me, perplexed. "Just say no."

"I can't. I promised, and apparently when a faery

promises something it can't be broken."

"But why did you promise to marry someone who isn't Adam?"

I sighed, at a loss for words. How could I explain it to Sierra? "The guy in charge threatened my life as well as the lives of everyone I love. So I had to, but now I need to find a way out of it. I love Adam. I can't marry someone else."

"Are you serious? He threatened you? Can't your dad take care of him?"

"I wish it were that easy." I was disgusted to feel tears well up in my eyes. "The faery world is beyond the reach of my dad's law enforcement."

Sierra touched my arm. "What can I do to help?"

"I have no idea." I turned my face away so she couldn't see the tears in my eyes.

"We'll figure it out." Sierra took a step towards me and then stopped. "Can I still hug you?"

"Duh. I'm still the same Rylie."

"Just with wings," Sierra said with a laugh and wrapped her arms around me. "Hey. Why are you crying?"

I spoke into her hair. "Happy that you're still my friend."

"Of course I'm still your friend. Don't be ridiculous." She squeezed me tight before letting go. She gave me a sympathetic smile.

For the first time since my life was completely inverted, I put to words a fear that had haunted me. "Do you think Adam will still love me?"

"He'd be an idiot not to. Like you said, you're still you."

I grinned at my best friend and counted myself lucky to have her support. She hadn't run screaming or judged me. As she always had, Sierra accepted me for me.

The problem was, I didn't really feel like me anymore.

CHAPTER FOUR

As soon as I walked through the door at school, I could tell something major was going on. Excitement lingered in the air. Everyone was huddled in corners whispering. I gripped Adam's hand and looked around curiously, wondering what could be so important. There'd probably been a school fight or something.

Sierra strolled up, her backpack slung over her shoulder. She didn't look quite as tired; maybe her nephew slept better last night.

"What's going on?" I asked.

She shrugged. "Apparently, the hottest boy ever just enrolled in our school, and cat fights are already starting. Five of the most popular girls have called dibs."

"All this over a boy? That's so stupid," I said with a laugh.

"That's not all. Rumor has it that he's excellent at sports—especially baseball." She looked pointedly at Adam.

"Is that so?" Adam looked around as if seeking out his competition.

"I doubt he's better than Adam." I squeezed his hand. Adam was very athletic; he'd already been accepted to a number of colleges on scholarship.

Adam let go of me to crack his knuckles. "I'll have to find this clown."

"You don't know he's a clown. He could be perfectly nice," I reprimanded and pulled Adam along to my locker. Guys were so competitive.

I had Adam, so I had no interest in the new guy. Let the other girls fight over him. Though I was slightly curious to see what all the fuss was about.

The whispers continued all morning, but I still hadn't gotten a glimpse of the new kid. I was starting to wonder if he actually existed until I walked into science and came face-to-face with the boy everyone was talking about.

Dressed in black like always, he fixed his familiar teal eyes on mine. I stopped in my tracks. Someone banged into the back of me, crushing my wings and propelling me forward a couple of steps, causing me to drop my books. The stack of folders, notebooks, and textbook hit the floor with a heavy thud.

Heart hammering in my chest, I took two shaky steps forward to pick up my books, but he was quicker. Kallan unfolded himself from the desk and stood with a fluid, graceful movement that made my heart skip a beat. I was unable to tear my eyes away from his beautiful face. His inky black hair was slightly longer than the last time I saw him, and his chest seemed wider. I could clearly see the muscles beneath his snug shirt. And his wings took my breath away.

Kallan picked up my books and offered them to me. His lip twitched slightly as if he was forcing himself not to smile. "You dropped these."

On autopilot, I took the books, our fingers brushing. This could not be happening. Kallan was the new boy everyone was talking about?

Without another word, Kallan turned away and sat back down.

I lowered myself into my seat and turned my head slightly in his direction. His eyes were now fixed on the chalkboard. I clasped my hands together in my lap to keep them from shaking.

Mr. Edwards walked in and nodded his head in Kallan's direction. "We have a new student. Please make sure he feels welcome."

All eyes turned to Kallan, and he smiled, completely at ease with himself and his surroundings. As Mr. Edwards started the lecture, Kallan lowered his head and flipped open his notebook with his long, slender fingers. I watched as he started to sketch. Although he didn't turn in my direction the rest of the class, I couldn't peel my gaze from him no matter how hard I tried. It seemed I wasn't the only one. Girls kept glancing back and smiling at him. He seemed oblivious to everyone in the room, including me.

I needed to get him alone to find out what he was doing there.

The bell signaled the end of class and Kallan stood up. He glanced back at me, a smirk on his face, and then went out the door. I gathered my books as fast as I could and followed after him.

When I burst into the hallway, I saw Kallan's head bobbing above a sea of students. I hurried after him, but as I got close, I noticed that Sarah, the head cheerleader, had her arm wrapped through his.

As much as I hated to admit it, jealousy coursed through me at the sight of another girl touching him. I wanted to tear her away from him and scream at her—completely disregarding the fact that I had a perfectly wonderful boyfriend and I wasn't supposed to even know Kallan.

My blood boiled. How dare he come disrupt my life without so much as an explanation?

"Rylie?"

I looked up, startled. Adam was standing in front of me, and the hall had almost cleared out. Another glance in Kallan's direction proved he'd disappeared from sight—him and Sarah.

"What are you doing? You're going to be late for class." Adam offered me his hand.

"Sorry. I guess I was daydreaming," I said absently.

Adam walked me to my class and gave me a puzzled look and a kiss before he headed off in the direction of his own. I was going to get the third degree later.

My mind raced. What in the world was going on? I scanned the classroom, but Kallan wasn't in this one, which was either a blessing or a curse. I wondered where he was and when he would talk to me. It was so hard to sit through the boring lecture. The teacher had to call my name three times before I realized she'd asked a question. One I didn't know the answer to, of course.

When the class was finally over, I walked to the lunchroom with Adam, Sierra, and Ian. Kallan sat at a table surrounded by girls, his hair so dark it looked like a starless night. Our eyes met; his gaze reminded me of the sea. Our wings both fluttered involuntarily at the same time.

"Rylie?" Adam tugged on my hand. "C'mon."

I sat down at our usual table and tried not to look

at Kallan sitting only feet away. Sierra watched me curiously.

"Can you get me a sandwich?" I asked Adam.

"Sure. Be right back."

Ian stood up with Adam. "Burger and fries?" he asked Sierra.

She nodded. "Don't forget the brownies."

Once they were out of earshot, Sierra turned to face me. "So you like the new boy, too?" When I didn't answer, she continued, "He is hot, but you should try to be a little more discreet around Adam. "

"What? No. That's...him." I kept my voice low.

"Him? Him who?"

I raised my eyebrows at her. "The faery."

"Get out of here. The one you're supposed to marry?" she hissed.

I nodded.

"What is he doing here?" She looked him over again. "And why didn't you tell me he was so gorgeous?"

I rolled my eyes and ignored her question. "I need to find a way to talk to him alone."

"Good luck with that. Every time I see him, he's flanked by girls."

"I've noticed," I mumbled under my breath.

Sierra cackled. "Rylie McCallister, are you jealous?"

I crossed my arms across my chest.

"Oh, boy." Sierra shook her head. "This is going to get messy, isn't it?"

I met her eyes. "I hope not. I love Adam. I can't hurt him."

Sierra's smile disappeared, and she leaned forward, her voice lowering. "I can see the way you're looking at this guy. There are feelings there, too."

I sat back and sighed. She was right. I did have feelings for Kallan—feelings I'd been trying to forget since the moment I left him and returned home. I didn't know what to do, but I did know I didn't want to be forced to marry anyone when I turned eighteen.

Later that day, I was at my locker switching out textbooks when I noticed a flash of black and teal. I jerked my head up in time to see Kallan disappear through the swinging door into the boys' room.

This was it. I slammed my locker door and leaned against the metal, watching as the warning bell rang and the halls began to empty. I didn't care that I would be late any more than Kallan appeared to. The second the last student jumped into their class, I made a bee-line for the restroom.

I paused outside the door, my hand on the wood as I had a last-minute worry that Kallan wouldn't be alone in there. Screw it, I thought, slamming my palm against the door.

Kallan stood in front of the mirror, washing his hands. His teal eyes glanced up at me, and then back down. A ghost of a smile crossed his lips. "This is the men's room, you know. Generally, that means no girls allowed."

I stalked across the room until we were side-by-side, and growled, "What are you doing?"

"Aren't you the one that told me about your wonderful human world?" Kallan asked, his voice quiet over the rush of the faucet. "I wanted to see for myself how 'awesome' it really was."

I narrowed my eyes at his reflection. "You hate the human world."

"My mother was killed here." He caught my gaze,

his lips pressed in a tight line. "So yes, I do hate it."

"Then why are you here, Kallan?" There was no longer any heat in my tone of voice, and I saw the way it affected him.

His entire face smoothed. He shut off the water and took his time drying his hands. When he finally turned to face me, he ran a hand through his hair. I could tell he was struggling with something.

"I'm here for you," he said softly. He lifted a hand, his fingers brushing my face as he stepped closer.

Panic struck me. I stumbled backwards, wide-eyed, and then clutching my backpack I raced out the door. "No. Oh, no."

"Don't run from me," Kallan said, following close on my heels.

In the empty, silent hallway, I whipped around and poked him in the chest. "I'm not due to return to you until next year."

Kallan opened his mouth to speak, but we were interrupted by a burst of giggling. I yanked my finger from his shirt as a group of girls rounded the corner.

"There you are!" Brenna called out. She was another cheerleader, with curly chestnut hair and huge brown eyes like a puppy's. She hooked an arm through Kallan's and smiled at me. "Hey, Rylie. Where's Adam?"

"I was about to go find my boyfriend right now," I said pointedly, my gaze locked on Kallan's.

"We need to talk," Kallan murmured.

I stepped back amidst the chatter of the girls around us. They weren't really paying any attention to us; I wasn't competition. Adam and I were *the* couple at school. "Sure looks like you have a lot of girls to choose from," I told him. "Maybe you could pick another."

"Rylie." He opened his mouth as if he had more to

say, but then clamped it shut.

Brenna moved in close to Kallan as if she was staking her claim. My heart was somewhere in my stomach as I hurried away, late for class and aching inside for the way life was easy before I was ever given wings.

CHAPTER FIVE

The second the last bell of the day rang, I was out of there. I didn't even go to choir, which I was sure to catch flak for later from Mrs. Lopez.

I didn't wait for Adam, either.

I couldn't face him. Not with my emotions so up and down, with my thoughts set to All Kallan, All the Time. Instead, I asked Sierra for a ride and then paced the floor until my parents got home.

Mom hadn't even put her purse down on the table before she sensed something was off. She eyed me warily. "What's wrong?"

No sense beating around the bush, I thought, and blurted, "Kallan was at school today."

Dad closed the door and shrugged from his suit jacket, his face thunderous. "He was at your school?"

"Not just at school, but enrolled." I resumed pacing. If I didn't stop, I'd wear a hole in the rug before the night was over.

"Did he say anything to you?" Mom asked gently.

"We talked for a minute." I threw my hands up in the air. "Something's up. I don't know what, and I don't like it."

Mom sighed. "I hate to say it, sweetie, but I think it's time to include Azura."

"Mom," I whined. I really didn't want to deal with Azura. Even though it had been almost a year, I still hadn't fully accepted her as my mother.

"She can help, Rylie."

"Fine! Is she still watching me? Do I go to the window and wave her in?" I asked sarcastically, and then contradicted myself by sitting at the table and letting my head fall into my arms.

"Don't be silly," Mom said. "She gave me a cell phone number to call."

Dad grunted. "She has a cell?"

"Yes." Mom picked up the phone and dialed a number.

As she talked, Dad took the chair beside me and put an arm around my shoulders. "Don't worry, hon. We're gonna figure this out."

I smiled. "Thanks, Dad."

An hour later, there was a knock at the door. My mother glanced between me and my father and quietly said, "I know neither of you are happy about this, but we need help. I expect you both to be on good behavior."

I pursed my lips, but nodded. Dad did the same.

Mom stood up and walked to the back door. Opening it, she said, "Good evening, Azura. Please come in."

"Thank you, Angela. You have been most kind to me even after everything I did."

"Aren't we all just victims of circumstance?" my mother responded gently, but her eyes were pinched as she led Azura into the living room.

It still amazed me that this seemingly young woman was my mother. Azura's hair was a shade lighter and a little longer than mine. Her green eyes matched her light green wings, and she wore a long, flowy dress that made her look like a hippie.

"Max," Azura greeted my father. Then she turned to me. "Oleander, you look beautiful. It's so good to see you."

I cringed as she called me by my faery name. "Thanks."

Azura sat down in the armchair across from the couch where my dad and I were seated next to each other. She leveled her gaze on me. "I understand that something has happened?"

I took a deep breath. "Kallan showed up at my school. He's glamoured and attending classes."

Shock and confusion crossed her face for a brief moment before she composed herself. "I don't understand. He's taking classes in a human school?"

"Yeah."

"Have you spoken to him?"

I nodded. "He said he was here for me. So, what does that mean? I have an entire year until I'm supposed to return."

Azura sat back in her chair. "I'm not sure. Let me think." She closed her eyes and remained very quiet.

I looked between my mother and father. Mom shrugged and Dad sat with his ankles and arms crossed. I rolled my eyes. This was ridiculous. What was she going to do? Wave her arms and make things go back to normal?

Azura lifted her head and shook it. "I'm sorry. I

have no idea why he would do such a thing. I can't believe his father even allowed it. Dark faeries are not my favorite by a long stretch, but they always keep their word. Maybe he wants to see you in your natural environment."

"That's all you've got?" I asked, aghast. "I thought you were going to be of some help."

My father stared at Azura, his face passive. "I think I should have a talk with this boy."

"Dad, no. At least let me talk to him again and see if he'll tell me what's really going on. If Azura is right, he can't make me leave."

"You're damn right he can't."

"The dark faery being here just doesn't make sense to me. I'm sorry I can't help you more." Azura leaned far over to put her hand on mine. "Oleander, I know you have been avoiding me, but you really need to come see your world. We have seers that might know what is going on."

I glanced over at my mother, and she nodded. She had been pushing me for a long time to learn more about my heritage.

"I don't like it. How do we know she would be safe with you?" My father leaned forward, his forearms resting on his legs. The look he gave Azura held no doubt that if she were to bring me to harm, he'd hunt her down.

"Oleander would only be on sacred ground," Azura assured him. "There is no way any one of the dark would try to take her. I promise you, she would be safe."

"Hello?" I snapped, looking between the three of them. "Stop talking about me like I'm not here. It's my decision to make."

All three relented, Dad holding his hands up,

Azura nodding, and Mom smiling.

I caught Azura's eye. "Do you really think there is someone who could help me?"

"Yes, Oleander. As you know, I cannot lie."

I crossed my arms over my chest and mulled the idea over in my mind. Truth be told, I was curious about what the light faery land would look like compared to the land of the dark. Maybe it was time I faced the truth. I'd been trying so hard to convince myself I was a normal human, but there was no denying that I was a member of the fey.

"Fine, I'll go with you," I started, but I glared when Azura beamed at me. "But only for a little while."

When Azura's face lit up like that, if it was possible, she looked even more beautiful. She clasped her hands together at her chest. "Thank you, Oleander. You have no idea how much this means to me."

I sighed, already regretting my decision. Curiosity killed the cat and all. "When do we go?"

Azura turned behind her and looked out the window into the darkness, as if gauging the time. "Tomorrow when you get home from school. I promise to have you back by nightfall."

I looked to my parents for their responses, and even though Dad's face was pinched and Mom's eyes were worried, they both agreed.

"I think you certainly should, Rylie," my mother told me with a wry grin. "Azura tells me you have much to learn."

"Tell me about it," I breathed.

My mother stood up, signaling the meeting was over. "Thank you for your help, Azura. Don't forget we are meeting for coffee on Thursday."

Azura smiled sincerely and stood to clasp my mom's hands. "I'm looking forward to it."

"Coffee? Since when are you two best friends?" I stared at my mom with my mouth agape.

"We have kept in touch," Mom said, her voice stern. "If I was in Azura's shoes, I would hope she would do the same for me."

"She took our baby, for crying out loud!" Dad barked, his face turning beet red.

My dad was clearly just learning about this friendship, as well. I think we both felt the same way about it.

"Yes, I know that." Mom narrowed her eyes. "And she gave us Rylie. If she hadn't come around desperate for someone to take care of her biological child, we wouldn't have any child at all. I'm very grateful to her. There is no reason we can't all get along."

My father seemed at loss for words. "You should have told me," he finally muttered.

My mom walked Azura to the door. When she came back into the room, my father and I stared at her, neither of us saying anything.

"Oh, get over it. She's lovely." My mom turned her back on us and made her way to the kitchen.

I exchanged an irritated glance with my dad, and then we followed.

Mom pulled out a glass and poured herself iced tea. "I've been telling you to give her a chance, Ry. It's really hard for her that you won't let her in your life. I can't even imagine what she must be going through."

"How long have you been meeting her?" my father asked with an edge to his voice. "And why the secrecy?"

"Since Rylie came back. I wasn't really keeping a secret. I always told you I was meeting a friend for coffee or lunch. I knew you guys wouldn't understand. As a mother, I feel very bad for Azura. She sacrificed her daughter for her safety. You can't begin to imagine how hard that had to have been for her. I guess it's my way of repaying her."

Dad walked up behind her and put his arms around her. "I wish you had told me."

"You never want to talk about it. Both of you just want to act like none of this is going on." She trained her eyes on me, her knuckles turning white as she grasped the glass. "Well, time is ticking, and you'll be eighteen before we know it. We need to face this reality, no matter how bizarre it is."

Dad sank into a chair, but didn't reply.

"I can't talk about this," I muttered, pivoting on the balls of my feet.

"Rylie!" my mom called after me. "Please don't be mad at me."

I turned slowly and shook my head. "I'm not mad. I just want to be alone."

I still couldn't believe Kallan had showed up at my school. What did it mean? Azura said it didn't make sense to her. That meant he didn't come because of my promise to him. If dark faeries always kept their word, they wouldn't force me to go early.

I trudged into my room and threw myself onto the bed in the dark. My only hope would be that someone I'd meet tomorrow might be able to help. I yawned and felt my eyelids getting heavier. I had homework to do, but I was too tired to do it right then, so I closed my eyes.

CHAPTER SIX

The alarm woke me at six a.m., and I groggily hit the button to dismiss it as I rolled out of bed.

The minute I stood, my wings sprang open, and I flapped them a few times. They liked to be stretched first thing in the morning, just like it felt good to stretch my arms and legs. I hurried through my shower and didn't waste time standing in front of my closet. I grabbed a pair of white jeans and an off-the-shoulder red shirt.

I took the stairs two-by-two and plopped down at the kitchen table, where I took my workbook and pencil out of my backpack and began doing homework. After a few problems, I peeled a banana and crammed it in my mouth.

"Slow down, Rylie. You'll choke," Mom said over my shoulder, the scent of her coffee wafting towards me.

"No time," I said, my voice muffled from the banana.

"Don't talk with your mouth full," she scolded.

I rolled my eyes. Mothers.

"Homework?"

"Yeah."

"Did you forget it?"

"I just didn't get to it last night. I fell asleep."

"Oh. Okay. I'll let you finish." She tinkered around the kitchen, making herself breakfast. She was a teacher at the local elementary school, so she usually left around the same time I did.

Sierra's horn honked before I was done with my homework.

"Did you finish?" Mom asked, giving me a stern look over her toast.

The progress report thing. She was going to ride me hard until I got my grades up. I smiled. "It's okay, I'll finish before class.

"All right..." she responded, the tone of her voice telling me "you better."

On the ride to school, I leaned back against the seat and tried to relax. My shoulders were already tense just thinking about if Kallan would be there again, and what we would say to each other.

"You're quiet," Sierra observed.

"Thinking."

"About Kallan?"

"Yeah. I don't understand why he's here."

Sierra signaled to turn out of my neighborhood. "Can't you ask him?"

"I tried." I sighed, watching my favorite department store whiz past, dark and silent so early in the morning. "His answer was cryptic and then we were interrupted."

"Ask him again."

"I plan to. But what if he's here to take me back?"

"Don't you think he would have done that already?"

I shrugged. It wasn't like he'd had that many opportunities to force me back to his world—I'd only just seen him for the first time yesterday. If that was what he wanted, he didn't have to go to my school to make it happen. He and his father could use brute force or even dark magick to bring me back, which was why I was certain there was more to this than met the eye.

"I don't like not knowing," I said as we took the curve into the school parking lot.

"Well then talk to him."

Sure, I needed to talk to him. But she made it sound so easy.

Adam was waiting for me near the front door, as usual. "Hey, beautiful."

"Hey, yourself."

"What's wrong?" He pressed a kiss to my forehead and squeezed my shoulder. "You looked upset."

I made a face as we went through the front doors. "I didn't get a chance to do my homework last night."

Oh, and the dark faery prince I'm promised to marry sits next to me in history class. Right, because I could tell him what was really on my mind.

"Bummer." He turned over his wrist to study his watch. "Looks like you've got about twenty minutes if you get to your first class ASAP."

"That's my plan. Not even gonna hit my locker." I patted my backpack.

Adam tossed an arm over my shoulders. "Hey, so was something going on last night? You usually call or text, and you didn't."

"I was tired. I fell asleep." I grimaced. "I'm sorry."

"It's okay. I was just a little worried."

"You could have called me."

"I didn't want to bother you."

"Next time, call." I stopped in front of my first period class and pecked his lips.

He laughed. "Okay."

Just then, a flurry of loud voices burst through the hallway, and I glanced over Adam's shoulder to see Kallan rounding the corner with a bunch of girls around him. He was smiling and talking, but something in his eyes told me he wasn't enjoying the attention like he was pretending to.

I didn't stop to think what I was doing. I turned back to Adam and stood on my tiptoes, sliding my arms around his neck and planting a long, hard kiss to his lips. The heated kiss was just the wrong side of passion for school, but luckily my teacher wasn't around.

When we broke the kiss, Kallan had passed us.

"I love you," I whispered, teasing my fingers through Adam's hair.

"I love you, too," he replied. His hands tightened on my waist and he winked. "Do you want to study after school?"

I giggled. By "study" he meant "look at our books for a minute and then go make out."

"Heck yeah!" I said, tempted to kiss him again. Then last night rushed back and I groaned. "Oh, wait. I can't."

"Why?"

"I have..." I paused. "An appointment."

"With a doctor? Are you okay?"

"No. A lady."

"A lady?" Adam's brows knitted together and he stepped away from me. "Why all the secrecy, Rylie?"

He looked confused and rightfully so. I couldn't tell him the truth, but I couldn't lie to him either.

Crap. I sighed. "She wants to talk about my family."

"Your family?"

"I'm learning more about my heritage."

"Okay. Like your family tree or something?"

"Yeah, something like that." I sighed, relieved when he didn't press on.

Much like his first day, Kallan was always surrounded by girls. I wasn't even able to catch him alone in the bathroom like the day before, though there wasn't a time he didn't pass me and catch my eye. We seriously needed to have a chat, and I could tell he agreed, but the cheerleading squad wasn't helping. It would have felt so underhanded to Adam if I tried to find out where Kallan was staying so that I could go speak to him, but another day like today and I'd go mad.

I tried to stay focused on school but failed utterly. At three o'clock, Adam dropped me off at home.

"Who's that?" he asked, nodding at the porch.

Azura sat stiffly on the bench swing, her long blonde hair flowing down her back.

"That's the lady I have to talk to," I said, irritated that she was already here. I'd been hoping to escape the car and get Adam on the road before she showed up.

"Wow, I can tell she's family. She looks just like you." Adam hopped out of the truck and walked around to open my door.

Ugh. I really didn't want to be told that I looked like Azura.

After I stepped from the truck, I started to say goodbye to him there, but he took my hand and said, "I'll walk you up."

Great. Now I'd have to introduce them.

"Hi." I nodded at Azura as she stood to greet us. "Adam, this is Azura."

"Nice to meet you." He stuck out his hand.

They shook, and Azura inclined her head regally. "And you, as well."

There was a moment of silence. I wondered if Adam was waiting for me to tell him how the two of us were related, but there was no way that was going to happen. I spoke up before anybody else could. "Okay. Azura and I need to start talking, and you need to get home, Adam."

He nodded. "Call me later?"

"Of course."

He leaned over and kissed me lightly before heading back to his car.

Once he was gone, I turned to Azura. "Thanks for not saying anything I'd have to explain."

"Seems like a nice boy," she commented.

I scoffed. "Right. Because you can tell after two words."

"Just trying to bond with you," Azura said with a sigh.

I felt bad. "Sorry. Let me take my backpack inside, and I'll be right back."

The house was empty. I dropped my backpack to the comforter in my room, and tucked my cell phone into my pocket—then chastised myself. What use would it be in a different realm? I set it on the nightstand, took a cursory glance at myself in the mirror, and returned to Azura.

"Are you ready?" she asked with a sweet smile. "I'm so looking forward to introducing you to everyone."

"Everyone?" Oh, boy. I didn't like the sound of that.

We began walking towards the forest. I hadn't gotten anywhere near it since I walked out of it a year ago, leaving behind weeks in captivity and a sullen, heartbroken Kallan. As the shadow of the trees fell over me, my breathing quickened and my heart pounded. Memories of being captured and dragged to the dark faery realm came flooding back to me. I turned back to my house, a safe place, and wondered if I should just go home.

Azura put her hand on my shoulder. "It's okay. You're safe."

I didn't even want to know how she knew what I was feeling. "I don't like being back here."

"I understand." Azura's voice was calm. "I won't force you to come if you're not ready, but I would like you to."

I looked in her eyes. She had been so patient with me these past months. It was time for me to take responsibility. Turning back around, I gestured to the woods. "Let's try again."

Slowly, we walked to the tree line. Varwik's face flashed before me in my mind. I kept telling myself he wasn't really there, that I wasn't in danger.

Azura patted my shoulder. "Just remember, you're going to the light faery realm. They can't find you there."

I nodded.

"Are you okay?" Azura asked.

"Yes." My voice was shaky.

"I'm so sorry that I let you get captured like that."

My heart fell as guilt set in. "It wasn't your fault."

"I should have stopped it."

I placed my hand on Azura's shoulder and paused until she faced me. "I don't blame you. Varwik would have gotten to me somehow."

She wiped a tear from her face. "Did he hurt you?"

"No. It was just hard to be held captive there." I didn't want to go into details. Being locked away in Varwik's castle with nothing to amuse me but a paperback of a Shakespeare play was not my idea of a good time. I was lucky when they bothered to feed me or deigned to take me for walks, like I was some kind of pet. "It's okay, really. I just don't want to go back."

We began walking again. Azura said, "I will make sure you don't."

"That's why finding a way out of the promise I made is essential." I looked around at the forest. "Kallan told me that this was neutral land."

"It is."

"How can you be so sure that I'm safe here?"

"First, you and Varwik made a promise, and he has no reason to break that. Second, I have friends in high places." She looked upward.

I followed her gaze, but didn't see anything. Puzzled, I looked back at her and she just smiled.

I had a lot to learn about the faery realms

CHAPTER SEVEN

"How much further?" I asked, glancing around. We hadn't walked far, but I was curious.

"We're almost there." Azura held back the brush so it wouldn't hit me in the face as we crawled over a fallen tree.

"You promised my parents we would be back by nightfall."

"You must remember, time is different in the faery world."

"Oh, right." How could I have forgotten? It seemed like I had been trapped in the dark world for weeks, but it had only been a few days, because time moved slower in the human realm.

Azura stopped abruptly. "Give me your hand, Oleander."

I hesitated slightly before extending my hand in front of me. Her warm, slender palm grasped mine and suddenly I felt like I was falling.

I griped her tighter and looked around. It was as if I was watching a movie on fast forward, all colors and motions whipping by all around us, and it stopped as quickly as it began.

My stomach felt queasy as I attempted to gain my bearings. "Wow," was all I could manage to say. I tried to take in the beauty of the land, but it was overwhelming.

Everything was so clear and crisp. If it was possible, the light faery world was even more breathtaking than the dark. The colors were lighter, mostly pastels. The flowers and trees reminded me of rainbow sherbet. The sky was a pale pink instead of blue and there wasn't a cloud in sight.

My body felt like it was humming. "Why do I feel so weird?"

"It's your magick. It's stronger here."

The green underneath me looked inviting. I kicked off my shoes and wiggled my toes on the soft moss. It felt amazing as it squished between my toes, cool and mushy.

"I want to take you to our home." Azura smiled at my wiggling toes. "I have a room set up for you. I always have. As you grew up, I changed it to what I thought you would like."

Warning bells went off in my head. She had a room for me? Was she going to force me to stay? "I'm not staying."

"I know. Don't worry, I would never ask you to do something you didn't want to do. I just want you to see where you should have grown up and to meet your aunt and grandmother."

"I have family here?"

"Of course. You also have several cousins, but we probably won't have time for you to meet them on this visit."

Azura led me through a field of beautiful wildflowers. I hastened my step to keep up with her.

"What's that noise?"

"It's the flowers. They're happy you are here."

"They're singing?"

"More like humming," Azura said brightly, and then pointed off into the distance where a huge tree stood. "That's our house."

"A tree? You live in a tree?"

"Of course. Where did you think we would live?"

"I-I don't know. A house?"

"It is a house. You'll see soon enough."

It took another five minutes before we reached the massive tree. I was startled to see a doorknob at the front. Azura pulled open the door, and my mouth dropped to the floor.

Inside was breathtaking. I knew the tree was big, but I didn't realize how big. We walked into an open living room. It was decorated simply, but that only added to the beauty. Wildflowers ran up the "walls" and vines hung down, separating the living room from the kitchen.

A winding staircase was off to the left. Azura started to climb the stairs, so I followed behind her. When we reached the top she waved her hand to the right. "That's my room. Across the hall is the bathroom and straight ahead is your room."

My stomach clenched. Suddenly, I was very nervous and my palms grew clammy. I wasn't sure why it freaked me out so much. It just all seemed so real. Azura was my mother. I should have grown up in a tree among other faeries. In a tree!

She flung the door open and my hand flew to my mouth. The room was perfect. The walls were obviously wood. A large window was off to the right with a bench in front of the window. I could almost see myself lounging on it staring out the window or flipping through a magazine. A hammock swing hung in the corner.

The bed was a twin with big logs for the four posts. The blankets were white with teal and black polka dots, which automatically made me think of Kallan. I pushed the thought of him out of my mind and focused on the room. The coolest thing about it was the floor. It was covered with dark green moss. My toes seemed to want to jump out of my shoes again.

"What do you think?" Azura turned to me, her eyes lit with excitement.

"It's pretty cool." I walked forward and touched the lights that were dancing on the wall. "What is this?"

"Faery lights."

"It's beautiful." A burst of color made me grin.

There was a long silence, and she finally remarked, "I wish you had grown up here with me. I'm sorry, Oleander."

"Don't be. I have a great life."

She inhaled sharply and looked away. I felt bad for hurting her feelings, but she did give me away. She had to deal with the emotions that came with it. I shouldn't have to make her feel better. But I didn't want to hurt her either.

"My sister and mother will be here soon. I'm going to start dinner. I'll call you when they are here." With that, she turned and left me alone.

As soon as she was gone, I took my shoes off. The floor was softer than I could have imagined. I smiled and scrunched up my toes like I had done on the beach many times before. It was a cool and comforting feeling.

After enjoying it for a few minutes, I looked around the room, taking in the smaller details. I ran my hand over the blanket on my bed. It felt smooth and cool, like satin. There were two fluffy pillows at the head of the bed. Opposite the bed was a six-drawer dresser with an oval mirror. The door next to the dresser opened to a closet. I gasped when I saw all the dresses lined up...by color. Azura must have known about my obsession with being organized. Or maybe it was hereditary.

I didn't care much for that thought.

I walked towards the bench and hesitated in front of it, as if sitting on it would force me to accept this life. Slowly, I sat down. The height of the bench was perfect for me to look out the window.

The bright green grass was sprinkled with patches of colorful flowers that extended as far as I could see. On the ground, faeries were walking around and playing in the last of the daylight. It was odd to see so many faeries together in one place. It wasn't like Varwik's castle at all. I had only seen a few there.

"Oleander!" Azura's sweet voice called to me. "Come on down. Please."

I swallowed hard. She wanted me to meet my grandmother and aunt, but I wasn't sure I was ready for that. What would they be like? What were they expecting from me? For some strange reason, I really wanted them to like me.

I descended down the staircase. My heart was beating so fast they could probably hear it.

An older woman and a woman who looked almost identical to Azura except for the length of her hair were waiting at the bottom on the stairs.

"Oh my! She's a beauty. As I knew she would be." The older woman who I assumed was my grandmother, although she didn't really look old enough to be, had a warm smile spread across her face. Her white wings had gold tips and her hair was such a light blonde it was almost white.

When I made it down the last step, the old woman pulled me into a tight hug. "Oleander, we have waited so long to see you. Thank you for coming." She pulled back, her hands on each side of my face as she stared at me for a long time in silence.

I cleared my throat. "Are you my grandmother?"

The woman laughed delighted. "Yes, I'm, as you say, your 'grandmother.' Here you would call me Móraí. But if you are more comfortable with Grandma or Nana, that's fine with me."

"Móraí. What does that mean?"

"It means 'old mother.'" She turned towards the other woman. "This is Lorella, your mother's sister."

I looked the young woman up and down and wondered if she was Azura's twin because they looked so much alike. Even their wings were the same light green color. "Are you twins?"

The woman laughed. "No, we are not twins. I am two years younger."

"You look so much alike."

"We hear that a lot," Azura said from the kitchen. "Why don't you all sit down? We'll eat and get to know each other better."

I was just glad for an excuse to move. I felt very self-conscious of the way the two of them kept staring at me.

"Do you need any help?" I asked, following the sound of her voice into a small, warm kitchen tucked into a small alcove of the tree.

"Sure." Azura stepped to the side where she was stirring a pot on the stove. "You can grab the bread out of the oven and put it on the table."

I grabbed a mitt from the top of the counter. The scent of the bread drifted into my nose, and I closed my eyes, wanting to remember it. I lifted the pan out of the old-fashioned oven. The light golden brown rolls looked so fluffy, I couldn't wait to sink my teeth into one.

I piled them on a nearby plate and walked over to the table, where Azura was pouring what looked to be beef stew into wooden bowls. My mouth watered. I hadn't realized how hungry I was. Azura nodded her head towards the chair next to her, so I walked around the table and sat down.

After a moment, the four of us settled around the table. I watched as Azura, Lorella, and Mórai clasped their hands in front of them. Were they going to pray?

"Mother Earth, thank you for this wonderful meal," my grandmother said softly. And then she dug in.

Quick and easy, I thought, smiling inwardly. I picked up my spoon and followed suit.

"Wow, this is delicious." I wiped my mouth with a napkin and felt a little twinge of guilt when I thought about my mom's horrible cooking. Azura obviously knew her way around the kitchen.

"Thank you." She smiled. "It's your Mórai's recipe. I will have to pass it on to you."

I picked at my roll and didn't say anything in response. I took after my other mother. I didn't like to cook, I couldn't cook that well, and I never really had any desire to learn.

"So your mother tells me that you are having some trouble in the human realm? The boy to whom you are promised has shown up unannounced?" Lorella raised an eyebrow.

I sighed and sat back in my chair. "Yup. I only got to talk to him for a minute. He said he's there for me, but I don't know what that means."

"Well, maybe Lorella can help," Móraí said, smiling. "She has the gift of sight."

"You can see the future?" I turned to stare at Lorella, surprised.

"It comes and goes, and it's not always accurate. It works best if I can actually touch the person, but sometimes I just get assaulted with images." She seemed modest about her gift. "Once we finish eating, I will try to get a reading off you, if you would like. Although sometimes, it's better not to know the truth. Some things are just meant to unfold as they will."

"I would like to know," I responded without hesitation. "It's driving me crazy."

After a dessert of fresh, delicious fruit, we cleared the table and washed the dishes, and then Lorella called me into the living room.

She sank to her knees. "Come. Kneel before me."

I lowered myself in front of her, my nerves dancing.

Lorella held out her hands. "Are you ready?"

Hesitantly, I placed my hands into hers. Lorella closed her eyes, so I did the same. I felt a sense of peace wash over me.

A couple of moments later, she pulled her hands from me. I opened my eyes to find a frustrated look on her face. "I'm afraid I am not much help. All I could see is a long winding road with a fork at the end. Your fate could go either way."

"That's it?"

"I'm sorry. As I said, some things have to work themselves out. I don't think your future has been decided."

"Well, what about Kallan? Did you see why he was there?"

Lorella smiled softly. "He is there because he can be nowhere else."

"What does that mean? He has to be there?"

"In a way, yes."

"Why are you being so cryptic?" I asked, annoyed. "Is he trying to take me back to his world? Is he going to kidnap me?"

"No, I didn't see anything like that. I don't think he is there to cause you trouble. As I said, he is there because he can't be anywhere else."

Well, that was a lot of help. I looked over at Azura and she shrugged.

Lorella stood up. "Just follow your path, Oleander. It will lead you where you are supposed to be."

I rolled my eyes. I could have gotten better advice from a fortune cookie.

CHAPTER EIGHT

Eventually, Móraí and Lorella left with promises to see me soon, and then I lay down in the hammock in my room for a catnap. Azura woke me sometime during the night, and we left the tree house twinkling behind us as we walked back through the woods.

The longer we walked, the lighter the night sky became. When we emerged, the sun was setting on the horizon.

"That's just weird," I mumbled.

"It takes some getting used to," Azura said with a laugh.

At the edge of the woods, I turned to face her and said, "Thanks for showing me your world. It was pretty cool," I admitted.

She studied me for a moment. "It's your world, too."

I nodded. "I'm beginning to see that."

"I hope you'll want to return."

"Soon." I smiled sincerely and walked towards my

house. My mind was trying to process everything, but it was just too much to take in. Part of me was angry that I didn't get a chance to grow up amongst other faeries. Another part was grateful for the life I had with my parents. Now I had to learn to balance both worlds.

I opened the door and yelled, "I'm home."

"In the living room," Mom called out.

My mom was sitting on the couch with a glass of iced tea in her hand. She grinned at me. "Hey. Have a good time?"

"Hey." I sighed and plopped down beside her on the couch. "Yeah."

My father looked at me over the newspaper from his favorite chair, face concerned. "Are you okay?"

"Yes. I'm fine." When he didn't stop staring at me, I added, "Really, Dad, I'm okay. It wasn't so bad."

"Why don't you tell us about it?" Mom asked.

I filled them in on my night and meeting some of my relatives. Mom seemed interested to know everything, but Dad looked like he wanted nothing to do with it.

"Are you hungry?" My mom went to stand up.

"No. I ate there."

"Oh." Mom looked a little disappointed. "Tired?"

"No. Just slept, too."

"Really?" She scrunched up her nose.

"Yeah. I was gone about four hours, right?" I looked at my father for confirmation.

"About that."

"That's like twelve hours there."

Dad sat up. "Where did you sleep?"

I hesitated, not wanting to upset my parents. "Azura has a room for me. I slept there, in a bed."

Dad shot Mom a look. "I don't like this. We weren't

supposed to worry about this until she was eighteen."

"Things happen. We need to deal with it now," Mom said in a soothing voice.

"I'm not going to disappear on you, Dad." I felt bad for him. "I'll always be your little girl. I'm just trying to figure a way out of the promise."

His eyes glistened in the light. "I don't want to lose you."

"You won't, and no matter what, I'll always return to you guys." I turned to Mom. "You know what I could use?"

"What?"

"Some ice cream. With caramel and nuts."

A smile spread across her face. "I'll go get us all some."

We each ate a bowl piled high with ice cream and toppings while we watched a funny sitcom and tried to pretend we were a normal family. But when I finally said goodnight and went upstairs, I found it hard to concentrate on my reading homework.

Azura, Lorella, and Móraí. What other relatives did I have? Girls my age? Little cousins under ten? I tapped a pencil on my notebook and realized it didn't matter—whoever they were, I wanted to meet them.

The faery world was so different from the human world. Both were wonderful in different ways. I felt like I was being pulled in opposite directions. I wasn't sure what I wanted anymore.

When Sierra picked me up the next morning, I jumped in the car bursting with excitement. "I went to the faery world last night," I blurted out, loving the fact that I could tell her.

"You did what?" She turned off the radio as she

pulled onto the road. "Tell me everything."

"Azura took me to her house, which was actually a tree, but a house."

"You're confusing me."

"She lives in a tree!" I laughed. "But once you're inside, it looks like a house. She had a room for me, and it was beautiful, Sierra."

Her eyes flicked to me. "You seem okay with everything, better than okay."

"I guess I'm finally accepting that the faery world is also my home. Not that I want to go live there forever or anything. I just understand now. That's where I'm from."

I gave her a breakdown of my night and everything that we said and did. By the time I was done talking, the car was already turned off in the school parking lot and Sierra was watching me raptly.

"It sounds amazing!" she said.

"I wonder if I could take you there sometime."

Her eyes lit up. "Do you think you could? Is that even allowed?"

"Kallan told me it was rare for humans to cross over to faery world, but not impossible."

"Speaking of..." Sierra trailed off and bit her lip. "Have you decided what you're going to do about Kallan?"

"I don't know. First thing I need to figure out is why he's here."

"How are you going to do that?"

"Ask him. He has to tell me the truth. Faeries can't lie."

"None of them?" she asked.

"Nope."

"Not even you?"

"No." I laughed at the excitement in her voice.

I didn't like the devilish glint in her eye as she tapped her chin and murmured, "Interesting."

I realized I probably shouldn't have told her that when I hopped out of the car and started thinking about all the things she could ask me.

Halfway across the front yard of the school, someone came up behind me and covered my eyes. For a brief second, I panicked, wondering who it might be. Then I recognized Adam's modern, masculine smell. I giggled and spun around.

We hugged, and his breath tickled my forehead as he said, "Hey. You didn't call me again last night."

I swore inwardly. "I'm sorry. I got caught up with Azura."

That was two days in a row I'd had to apologize to him. I felt horrible. This wasn't like me at all.

"Azura?" He wrinkled his nose. "I can't get used to the sound of that name."

"Yeah. I know it's a strange one," I said brightly, but thought, As if Oleander is any better.

"I guess you'll have to make it up to me." He gave me his contagious, crooked grin.

I laced my hand through his as we entered the building and walked down the long, narrow hallway. Someone banged into my wings, and I glared at them as I pulled them away. "How can I make it up to you?" I asked my boyfriend.

"Let's hang out after school. I feel like we haven't been spending enough time together."

I smiled. "I'm sure that can be arranged."

"Did you enjoy hanging out with that woman?" he asked.

"Yeah," I admitted. "It turned out to be okay. It's interesting to learn about my family history."

I put my backpack in my locker and turned to

face Adam. His eyes locked with mine, and I could see the love in them. My heart melted. I leaned against him for a minute, listening to his heartbeat.

"You okay?" he asked.

"Just hold me for a minute. I've missed you, too." I closed my eyes and tried to relax.

He wrapped his strong arms around me and squeezed, then gently pushed me back and ran his thumb down my cheek. Softly, he touched his lips to mine. The kiss started off slow, and then turned more intense. When he finally pulled away, I was out of breath.

"I'll see you later," Adam whispered in my ear.

"Okay." I bit my bottom lip.

After he left, Sierra took a couple steps towards me. "Well, that was...different," she said, searching for the words.

"Mmm." I could only agree.

On the way to my first class, I spotted Kallan in one of the common areas where a dark-haired girl stood next to him, her fingers running through his hair.

Jealousy coursed through my veins, but I quickly chided myself. Wasn't I just doing the same thing with Adam? When Kallan helped me escape his world, I told him it was because I wanted to go back to my human life and be with Adam. So why was all the attention Kallan received upsetting me? I had no claim to him. In fact, I was trying to find a way out of this mess.

Kallan looked up and our eyes met. I pursed my lips, spun around, and walked away. Sierra chased after me without saying a word. We took a left down a side hall to English class, and for an entire hour, I gnawed on my pen as I thought about how to get

Kallan alone and exactly what to say to him. I went through all sorts of scenarios in my head. The bell startled me out of my thoughts, and I glanced down at my notebook—I hadn't taken any notes.

I sighed, mad at myself. I had no idea what the teacher had talked about in class. Hopefully there wouldn't be a quiz.

My day only got worse when I saw Kallan again in science class, smiling as a different girl stroked his arm and batted her eyes. I marched past him and took my seat. Once again, the teacher's lecture was completely useless as I watched him and her steal glances at each other.

During lunch, I sat with Sierra and Adam. "Where's Ian?" I asked in an effort to make conversation instead of mooning over Kallan.

"I don't think he'll be sitting with us today."

"Why not?"

"Things aren't working out." She popped a grape in her mouth.

"Oh, Sierra. I'm sorry." I touched her hand.

"It's okay. We're friendly. I'd rather it end like that than in a fight."

"So you don't need me to beat him up?" Adam asked, his chest puffing up like a rooster. I rolled my eyes but laughed anyway.

Sierra chuckled. "No. That's okay. But thanks for offering."

"There had to be a reason?" I couldn't believe she hadn't told me earlier. I've been a lousy girlfriend and a poor friend lately.

She shrugged. "He was more into me than I was him. He dropped the L-bomb and it freaked me out."

I thought back to when Kallan had surprised me in front of his father by claiming he loved me. I glanced over at his table and found him staring back at me, the cluster of girls around him chatting and laughing. My wings fluttered. Whenever he was around, it was as if I was hypersensitive. Just being in the same room as him made me flustered.

I couldn't get out of the cafeteria fast enough. Somehow, I made it through the rest of the day, rejoicing when the bell rang. I got what I needed from my locker and as I walked with Adam to his truck, I felt Kallan's eyes on me.

"Where are we going?" I asked when Adam and I were settled in the cab.

"It's a surprise," he responded.

"What is it?"

"If I told you, it wouldn't be a surprise."

"I know. I know."

It didn't take me long to realize that we were heading towards the lake. It was a half hour drive from where we lived and a popular hang-out spot.

Adam parked and helped me out of the truck. After shutting the door, he said, "We haven't been spending a lot of time together. I thought maybe we needed to get away for a couple hours."

I hugged his waist. "It's perfect."

We walked along the banks, stopping every once in a while to kiss or throw rocks in. We found a spot under a large tree to sit and watch the sun set, our arms wrapped around each other.

Just as the sun went down past the horizon, I turned and cupped Adam's smooth face in my hands. "I love you."

He grinned. "I love you, too."

Our lips touched, sending shivers down my body. His hands moved up my back and then down my arms, holding me close. Our lips parted, the kiss deepening.

After a few more minutes, we broke apart and smiled shyly.

That kiss had been exactly what I needed to get my head on straight again.

CHAPTER NINE

I woke up and the first thing that crossed my mind was Kallan. So much for Adam's kiss.

I tossed my pillow across the room. He was driving me crazy. I had to find out why he was here, and it had to be today. I couldn't stand not knowing. I got ready for school in record time. I knew it shouldn't matter, but I made an extra effort to look nice. I turned side to side looking at myself in the mirror. The long skirt reminded me of the flowy clothes I'd worn in the dark world.

I found Kallan standing near his locker. There were two girls beside him making goo-goo eyes, but I didn't care. I had a plan now. I marched up to him and looked him in the eyes.

I had a gift; I might as well use it. My gift was that I could use anyone else's power as long as they were nearby. Kallan's power was mind control, so when I was near him, I could use mind control, as well.

Meet me out back near the basketball court. Wait a couple of minutes before you follow behind me.

Kallan's eyes widened in surprise.

I turned and walked away without speaking a word out loud. The two girls probably thought I was crazy. Whatever.

Outside, I ran my hands along the chain-link fence while I waited for him to arrive. When I heard the door open, my heart fell to my knees. Suddenly, I was really nervous about being alone with him. Maybe this wasn't the best idea.

He strode out onto the court, both hands shoved into his pockets. He stopped in front of me, his face impassive. "I take it you willed me out here? One minute I'm standing at my locker in a conversation with other people, and the next I'm rushing out to a basketball court and missing my class."

I shrugged. "It was the only way I could get your attention."

"You always have my attention." His eyes met mine, and it was obvious he wasn't joking. Our wings fluttered.

His admission totally caught me off-guard. Focus, Rylie. "You said you were here for me. What does that mean? Are you here to take me back?"

"No. I'll wait until you're eighteen. You have a deal with my father."

"Then why are you here? Why are you flirting with these other girls?"

"Are you jealous?" He raised his eyebrow.

I pressed my lips together, determined not to say anything.

"Well? Are you?" He wasn't going to let it go.

"Yes," I spit out. "Happy?"

"No." His face softened. "I don't want you to hurt."

"Are you just trying to make me miserable? I was supposed to have this time with my friends."

Kallan looked away. "And Adam."

"Yes, and Adam."

When he answered, his voice was low and apologetic. "I wanted to have a chance to prove to you that I'm the right guy for you. You don't belong in this world, Oleander."

I bristled. "Kallan, this is my world. And my name is Rylie."

"I'm not going to get in your way, but I'm also not giving up either." He touched my hand at my side, and the electricity that pinged through me from that small, brief connection made me feel guilty. "I love you, and I'm not walking away. I've been going crazy since you left."

"You know I can't get out of the promise."

"I want you to come back on your own free will, not because of my father. Please, Ol—Rylie, just give me a chance."

I felt too stifled by his presence, and took a step away. "I have a boyfriend, you know that."

"Yeah, I know. Believe me, I know." Kallan ran his hand through his coal-black hair. "I don't know what I'm doing here. I can guarantee this is much harder for me than it is you. But it's like something is pulling me here. I know it sounds crazy, but I can't be anywhere else but here."

My heart stopped, and I fought the urge to take another step back. That was kind of what Lorella had said when she looked into my future. "What did you say?"

"You heard me," Kallan said as he took a step closer and laid his hand on my arm, sending warmth racing through my body.

I inhaled sharply. I almost forgot the effect his touch had on me. "Kallan, I can't."

He pulled his hand away. "I won't force you. All I ask is that you spend some time with me. Get to know me a little better."

A loud creak of the door startled us both, and a teacher poked her head out. She was middle-aged, with graying hair pulled up in a tight bun. I didn't recognize her. Upon seeing us, her brow furrowed and she opened the door wider. Just our luck.

"What are you two doing out here?" she barked. "Report to the principal's office, both of you."

Kallan turned and stared at the woman for a long moment. Her knitted brow loosened and her face smoothed, then she walked back inside.

"What did you tell her?" I whispered, taking a deep breath as he finally let go of me.

He smiled, his teal eyes sparkling. "Nothing major. I just wiped the memory of seeing us. As far as she's concerned, we were never here."

"Thanks. My parents would have killed me if they knew I got sent to the principal's office." My hand was still tingling from his touch. "I can't even imagine the mischief you got away with because of your power."

"If you give me a chance, I'll tell you all about it."

His statement gave me pause. I was supposed to spend the rest of my life with this guy if Varwik had his way. It couldn't hurt to get to know him a little better. It wasn't like I was going to cheat on Adam. Just talking.

"Maybe."

"That's a lot better than hell no." Kallan pulled his cell phone out of his pocket. "What's your number?"

I hesitated and then reached for the phone and entered my number. Our hands brushed when I handed the phone back. I felt more alive when I was around Kallan, as if all my senses were heightened.

Adam, I reminded myself. I loved Adam.

"I'll text you," Kallan told me.

I nodded and hurried away, scared of what I'd just done.

As soon as we were settled in the car after school, Sierra narrowed her eyes at me. "Spill."

"Huh?"

"What's going on with you today?" she asked. "First you were late for class, then you barely spoke a word at lunch. And when Adam asked if you wanted a ride, you totally brushed him off."

I groaned. "Did I?"

"Don't change the subject." Sierra threw the car into gear and shot out of the parking spot. "Answer my question."

"I talked to Kallan," I admitted.

"And?" she prodded.

"He wants me to get to know him better."

She eyed me. "That's it? That's his master plan? Hang out and get to know each other?"

"Eyes on the road!" I yelled, grabbing the door handle as she veered towards the curb.

"Who's driving this car?" she quipped, sticking her tongue out at me. "Are you gonna? You know, 'get to know him.'"

"There's no harm in talking to him." I didn't know if I was trying to convince her or me.

"You sure about that? It could lead to trouble."

I shrugged. "I'm not sure about anything anymore."

"I sense a broken heart in someone's future."

I groaned. She was right. One way or another, someone was going to get hurt.

We said goodbye in my driveway and I went inside, where I sat at my desk trying to get some homework done. My math was already overdue and science was due tomorrow. I needed to get all of it done.

I worked for some time, barely noticing as my parents came home, until Mom poked her head into my room. "Rylie?"

"Yeah?" I didn't bother to look up.

"Azura is here."

"I've got a lot of work to do," I said, motioning to the stacks of work scattered across my desk. "Can she come back tomorrow?"

"I think she just wants to talk for a minute."

I sighed and dropped my pencil, annoyed at being interrupted. "Okay, fine."

Mom held the door open, and Azura walked in. Great, so she'd heard my annoyance. I was definitely going to yell at Mom for that later.

"I won't keep you long, Oleander," Azura said softly. "I wanted to invite you to a festival this weekend."

"A festival?"

"We are celebrating the spring equinox. It's an important day for us: one of the two times a year that the sun is in complete balance."

I had so much to learn about the faery world. It seemed like lately, everything Azura said intrigued me. I was totally curious about their customs. "When is it?"

"Saturday. I'll come get you. It will be a lot of fun, and you can meet your cousins."

"Okay." I nodded, even though I wasn't sure how I felt about having cousins.

She grinned happily. "Wonderful! I'll see you

then."

I went back to work until my cell phone dinged. I slammed my pencil down in frustration; all these distractions weren't helping the fact that I hated homework.

I knew immediately the text was from Kallan because it was so formal.

Could we see each other tonight?

For once, I was crazy happy to have so much homework. *2 much hw.*

Hw?

Homework.

His texts took longer than Sierra's or Adam's—probably because it was his first time ever handling a cell phone, much less texting. *When will you be finished?*

IDK

?

I laughed to myself. *I don't know. I'll text u back.*

Okay.

It took another hour to finish my homework because I started thinking about seeing Kallan alone. Just the thought completely broke my concentration.

Feeling just a tiny bit guilty, I picked up the phone and texted Adam first. I told him I was done with my homework and I'd see him tomorrow. At least I remembered that.

Then I texted Kallan. *Done but it's late. Maybe 2mrw?*

Can't I see you now?

I groaned out loud. I thought I had the perfect excuse to postpone. *It's dark.*

Please.

K. Meet u out back.

I peeked in the mirror to make sure I looked okay,

then ran a brush through my hair and fixed my outfit. It was late, and I knew my parents wouldn't let me out, so I'd have to use my glamour to turn invisible and sneak out the back door.

They were in their room watching TV. I willed myself invisible and snuck down the stairs and into the kitchen. I paused at the back door, listening for any sign they might have heard me. Carefully, I turned the knob and went outside.

The air was brisk and felt good on my skin. I willed myself visible again and looked around. I didn't see Kallan yet. I wasn't sure where he was coming from. Did he go back into the woods at night? Back home? Or was he staying somewhere in the human world?

Shortly after, I saw a figure near the woods. Since faeries had better sight than humans, I knew immediately it was Kallan. His wings practically glowed in the dark. My heart flip-flopped as I walked towards him. His eyes glistened in the moonlight. I fought the urge to run to him and throw my arms around his neck.

"Hi," he said shyly.

"Hey." I nervously pulled at the hem of my shirt.

"Lot of homework?"

"Yeah. I haven't been keeping up lately. I need to catch up or my parents are going to ground me."

"That sucks. They give out way more homework here than in my world. Our classes are mostly interactive so we do the work at school."

"That's cool."

"Do you always struggle with school or is this something new?"

"I've never been a straight-A student, but I usually keep up with the work and get decent enough grades."

"Oh. I hope it's not because of me?"

I wrapped my arms across my chest. "In a way.

I've had a lot on my mind since you brought me home."

"I'm sorry. I can help you catch up, if you want."

"It's not just your fault. It's mine for not getting through this better." I sighed. "Let's not talk about school. Okay?"

"Sure, what do you want to talk about?"

"You want me to get to know you better, so tell me something I don't know."

"Okay." He laughed and tapped his finger to his lips, thinking. "I like puzzles."

"Puzzles? Like jigsaw?"

"Yes. I like figuring out how to put things together."

"Are you good at the Rubik's Cube?"

"What's that?"

It was my turn to laugh. "Just a game. Forget it." I looked up at the stars. "Where are you staying?"

"Close by," he answered vaguely.

"Are you staying in the human realm or going back and forth every day?"

"I have a place here, but I go back a lot to check in."

"I'm sure your father is not thrilled..."

"He thinks I'm showing weakness."

"Weakness? How so?"

"Come on. Look at me. I left my home, my school, my friends—to be near you."

My skin rippled with goose bumps at the look in his eyes. "And that's showing weakness?"

He shrugged and looked off in the distance. "Well, if it is, it's worth it to me."

"Oh." I didn't know what else to say. It tripped me up when Kallan was honest with his feelings, considering how good he was at being evasive. It was weird to be in a relationship where neither person could lie.

"Your turn. I told you I like puzzles. Now you tell me something. Where do you like to vacation?"

"The beach is nice. We always go there on family vacations. Have you ever been there?"

"Not in your world."

"I should take you sometime. The water isn't as clear as yours, but it's still beautiful. There's something relaxing about the sound of the ocean waves."

"I'd like to see your world with you."

His words always had a way of disarming me. I wanted to be angry at him, but it was impossible.

We walked along the tree line. "You sure are popular with the girls at school."

"You are more beautiful than any other girl at that school."

I was glad it was dark and he couldn't see me blush. "I think you're biased, because you can see my wings, but thanks."

"Wings aside, those girls still don't hold a candle to you." He stopped in his tracks and turned towards me.

We gazed into each other's eyes. Kallan's hand brushed mine. I jerked it back. "Kallan…"

"Rylie…" Kallan backed me up against a tree. I could feel his breath on my neck. My heart pounded in my chest. He ran his hand down one of my wings, sending a jolt through my body. "I…"

I reached up and softly touched Kallan's cheek. "I can't."

"Adam?"

"Yeah."

He let go of me. "I'll walk you back to your house," he said, looking down at the ground.

"I'm sorry."

He was silent until we reached my back door. I

turned the knob and looked back to say goodbye, but he had disappeared.

CHAPTER TEN

"Morning," I muttered to Sierra when I got in the car, cringing as I accidentally slammed the door.

She grunted a response, her eyes squeezing shut.

"You okay?" I asked, noticing the music was off. That wasn't like her.

"Bad night."

"The baby?"

"Mhmm. On top of that, my head is pounding." She put the car into gear and pulled out of the driveway.

Something was definitely up with her, and I thought maybe it wasn't just about her nephew.

In the parking lot at school, Adam ran up to the car before we could even get out. His eyes danced in excitement. "Guess what?"

I smiled at his giddiness despite my bad mood. "What?"

"My parents are taking me to check out Southern

Cal over spring break."

"Really? That's awesome!" I threw my arms around him. Adam's dream was to get into Southern California to play baseball and from there, he hoped to make it to the major leagues. But California was a long way from Virginia. I planned on applying to a few schools in California, but with my grades the way they were, the chances of getting in were slim to none.

"I'm sure you'll have fun," Sierra chimed in.

I planted a big kiss on his lips. "I wish I could go with you."

"Me too." With his arm around me, we walked into the school.

Adam had baseball practice after school so Sierra dropped me off at home. I ran up the stairs two at a time and threw myself on my bed.

Kallan hadn't been at school. He wasn't in the class we shared, and the morose looks on the faces of the girls who usually flanked him proved he wasn't there.

I stared at the ceiling for a few moments and then pulled my phone out of my jeans before I could talk myself out of it.

R u ok? I typed and hit send.

I stared at the phone and willed a reply to come through, but it didn't. With a heavy sigh, I pulled myself out of bed and took my school books from my bag, thinking I might as well get some work done.

After a few minutes of reading passed, I realized I'd read the same paragraph over and over. It was too hard to concentrate because of Kallan. Why wasn't he at school? And then a thought hit me—maybe he decided to go home after last night.

My shoulders sagged. I was surprised at how sad that made me.

C'mon, Rylie, concentrate on your schoolwork. I sighed and focused harder on what was in front of me.

Two hours later, my phone chimed. My heart leapt, and I reached for my phone, but in my haste, I dropped it to the floor. I reached down under my desk to pick it up and whacked my head on the edge of the desk when I stood up.

Rubbing my head, I swiped the phone to see the message.

My heart sank when I saw it was Adam. *Practice sucked. I'm beat and heading home 2 sleep.*

Ok. C u 2mrw.

Love u.

Love u 2.

I threw the phone on my bed, irritated that a text from my boyfriend hadn't been as important to my stupid brain as a text from Kallan. Grumbling to myself, I went back to my books.

I was surprised when my mom yelled up that dinner was done, because I hadn't even heard them come home. I placed my pencil back in its spot and stood up.

I trudged down the stairs and shoveled watery mac and cheese down my throat, laughing inwardly as I wondered how anybody could screw up mac and cheese, but somehow my mother managed to. Not that I was any better. I could ask Azura to teach me, but I didn't enjoy cooking or baking.

After small talk about our day, I took my last swig of my soda and wiped my mouth, then excused myself to get back to science vocabulary. It seemed hopeless. I was never going to catch up.

Before I went to bed, I checked my phone one last

time.

No new messages.

A knock on the door woke me up the next morning. Sunlight filtered through the crack in my curtains, and I turned towards my door, rubbing my eyes.

"Rylie?" Mom said softly. "Azura is here to take you to the spring festival."

Crap. Was that today? I groaned. "Okay. Can you ask her to wait while I get ready?"

I heard some voices, and then Mom said, "Azura says you can get ready at her house. Just get presentable."

"Oh." I struggled to get out of bed. "Give me a few minutes."

The door closed, and I stretched my arms, legs, and then my wings. I blinked a few times, trying to wake myself up as I made my way down the hall to use the bathroom. I splashed water on my face and dabbed it dry. Even with the beauty that came with being a faery, I looked tired.

Back in my room, I took a short-sleeve blue shirt off the hanger and paired it with a pair of jean capris.

I stuffed my phone down in my pocket, took a look around my room to make sure everything was in place, and headed downstairs. Mom and Dad sat in the kitchen across from Azura.

"Morning," I said to the room. "Should I eat?" I directed my question at Azura.

"You don't need to. We'll be eating all day."

Not to mention the food was much better in the faery world.

Azura glanced at my parents. "Oleander is welcome to come back here anytime she wants, but the celebration will last well into our night."

"She has school Monday," my dad spoke up.

"And I have studying to do for tests." I didn't mind going to the fair, but I didn't want to be stuck there long. Especially since I hadn't heard from Kallan.

Azura turned towards me. "You can come back whenever you want, but if you want to stay for the whole festival, I'll have you back by Sunday morning so you have the day to study."

"Okay," I agreed tentatively.

Dad didn't look happy, but he said, "Fine."

I walked over to my parents and kissed both of them. "I'll be okay. I'm taking my phone. Leave me a message if you can't get through. I love you both very much."

"We love you too." Mom smiled. "Try to have fun."

"Yeah. Fun," Dad practically growled.

I wrapped my arms around him. "I'll be home soon."

Azura opened the door, and I followed her outside. "They'll be okay," she reassured me.

"I know. It just feels like I'm hurting them."

"That's understandable. They love you very much."

We headed towards the woods. Azura led the way again on a gently sloping trail. I was still unsure of where to go. "How do you know where you're going? The woods always seem the same."

"Well, I have been doing it for almost seventeen years." She cracked a smile.

I laughed. "Yeah, I guess."

"You'll find your balance soon. Try this. Just stand still right here." She took me by the shoulders. "Close your eyes and breathe."

I did as she instructed.

"What do you feel?"

"Warmth."

"Mhmm. What else?"

"Familiarity?"

"Good. Without opening your eyes, tell me, which way do we go?"

I pointed with my left hand.

"Perfect."

I opened my eyes, and we walked the way I pointed. "I got it right?"

"Yes. You will find yourself feeling more at home with nature. You can listen to the trees, the flowers, the piskies, whatever is around, and find your way home."

I knew by "home" she meant her house and not where I grew up.

She stopped a few minutes later. "Ready?"

"Are we going through that weird feeling area again?" I asked with a laugh.

"You'll get used to it."

I took a few deep breaths, remembering how odd it felt last time. "Ready."

Azura took my hand, and we continued. My stomach felt queasy, and I was glad I hadn't eaten breakfast. After a minute, it felt normal again, but when I looked up, the sky was dark and a million stars danced above. "Wow..." I murmured and took a minute to relish them. "When does the queasiness stop?"

"With time."

Of course. "What time is it?"

"Almost sunrise."

As we got closer to tree house, the sky turned different shades of pink and purple. "It's beautiful."

The yards were quiet at this time of the morning, but some light shone inside the other tree houses. Azura noticed me craning to see inside and laughed.

"We get up early for the celebration." Azura answered my question before I even asked it. She opened the front door at her house and let me walk in first. The sweet lavender scent tickled my nose. "Would you like breakfast? Or do you want to get ready first?"

"Um...whatever. It doesn't matter to me. I guess I can get ready while you cook?"

"Wonderful. There are dresses in your room and please feel free to use whatever you need to in the bathroom."

"Thank you."

Azura went to the kitchen, and I headed up the stairs.

My room was just the way I'd left it. I grabbed a robe from the closet and headed back down the hall for the bathroom, but I noticed this time that Azura's bedroom door was open. Curious, I poked my head inside.

It was sparsely decorated—whitewashed walls with a floral trim, a pale wood bed and matching dresser that held a vase of fresh lavender next to a picture frame. I glanced over my shoulder, noting the empty hallway, and walked inside to pick up the frame.

It was a baby picture—of me. It looked just like the one my mom had from the hospital, my tiny pink face poking above the soft blanket covered in butterflies that my mom had brought for me. This same picture still sat on the mantel in our living room.

"It was the only picture I could keep," Azura said from behind me.

I jumped and put the frame down before I whirled around, sheepish at being caught in her room.

"If I had other photos of you, someone might have found out." She smiled sadly.

"I didn't mean to pry."

"You're not prying. This is your home, too, Oleander."

I nodded, then with a flash of bravery, I touched her shoulder. "Thanks, Azura."

The shower had an overly large showerhead that sprinkled water light enough to not be too rough, but with enough output to not have to rinse my hair for ten minutes. The bathtub was huge and allowed plenty of room for my wings to expand. It was so much easier to shower here than it was at my house. I didn't have to keep my wings tucked in at all.

I dried off and examined the robe. It had slits so I could put it on around my wings. I popped a hand through the slit and realized that must have been how Kallan wore T-shirts all the time. They were made differently. I guess faeries had always done things differently.

I shrugged into the robe, the fabric settling perfectly around my wings. Had I grown up here, this stuff wouldn't seem weird. I would just know what to do. But then I would have never known my parents, Adam, or Sierra, I reminded myself.

When I stepped into the hall, Azura called, "Come eat before you get dressed, while the food's hot."

I sat at the kitchen table and she placed a big plate of French toast in front of me and a bowl of fruit in the center of the table. My mouth watered at the smell. I waited for her to sit down and say her thanks, then I picked up the fork and inhaled the French toast.

As I moved on to the fruit, I moaned, "This. Is. So. Good."

Azura grinned. "I'm glad you like it."

I smiled back and slowed my chewing. "I do. It's amazing. Thank you very much."

"Don't eat too much. There'll be a lot of food to try

at the celebration."

I nodded. "I can't wait."

There was a beat of silence before she caught my gaze and said, "I'm so happy you're here."

I wasn't sure how to respond. I liked being here—I mean, heck, I could shower without getting a wing cramp!—but I still wished all of this would disappear so I could go back to living a normal life. "How many cousins do I have?"

"Many."

"I'm not used to having a big family."

"I know." Azura set her fork down. "I'm sorry for that."

"Do you have more brothers or sisters? A father?"

"My father passed away a while ago."

"Sorry to hear that."

"Lorella is my only sibling. We grew up very close."

"That's nice." I had always wanted a sister. Sierra was the closest thing I had to one.

"Why don't you go get ready now?" Azura suggested with a hint of sadness in her voice. For the first time, I realized that Azura was alone all this time, and she never had any other children to keep her busy. She just watched and waited for me. That couldn't have been easy.

Back upstairs, I looked through all the dresses and settled on a sleeveless light blue dress that touched right above my knee. I couldn't believe how perfectly it fit. I searched the bottom of the closet for shoes, and then remembered faeries preferred not to wear them. I'd be going barefoot. I loved that.

I played with my hair a little, pulling the sides up out of my face, but leaving the back down. My face needed no makeup. I touched the necklace Kallan had given me. My fingers then moved to the bracelet from

Adam. I sighed. What was I going to do? Whatever happened, someone was going to get hurt. And I hated that. It wasn't fair.

No. Not today, I told myself. Think happy thoughts today. It's a celebration!

Azura knocked on my door. "Oleander! It's time to go."

Now if I could only get her to stop calling me that, I laughed to myself. That wasn't going to happen.

I opened the door and faced Azura. She gasped and tears formed in her eyes. "Beautiful."

I blushed. "Thanks. You look nice, too."

Azura was dressed in a short-sleeved green gown, longer than the one I was wearing, but not too long. She had put her hair up in a loose bun. She wore a single-stone necklace that matched her eyes—jade, maybe? I didn't know enough about crystals and stones to recognize them yet.

"Why didn't you ever remarry? You're gorgeous. Surely there have been men that want to be with you?"

She cast her eyes downward. "It was never important to me. After your father left... I just didn't want to go through that again."

"Not everyone is bad. There could be someone out there to make you happy."

"I am happy. Don't worry about me." She settled her face into a luminous smile. "Come. The celebration awaits."

CHAPTER ELEVEN

I followed Azura down the dirt trail in front of her
house. The crude road was lined with huge grass
yards and tall tree houses similar to Azura's. Just a
little earlier all was dark and quiet, but now everything was full of life. There was so much beauty to
take in. I hoped I never got used to being in awe of the
faery world.

Faeries were busy decorating and preparing for
the celebration, setting up tables and feasts, while
piskies hovered around—right out in the open.

"Kallan once told me not to follow the piskies," I
told Azura, just to make conversation as we walked.

She laughed. "A good piece of advice, to be sure.
They aren't bad creatures, necessarily, just lackadai-
sical. They'll make you feel happy and free, and you'll
disappear with them in the forest to dance your life
away."

We stopped a few houses down where a group of
faeries were stringing up colorful lights.

"Morning, ladies," Azura said brightly.

They all turned and greeted Azura, and then looked at me. I suddenly felt like I was on stage and the spotlight was pointed directly at me.

I swallowed hard and managed a meek, "Hi."

All four sets of eyes shifted to my birthmark. I thought of some sarcastic remarks to make, but held them back. I didn't want to embarrass Azura or myself.

After another moment of awkward silence passed, the faery with green wings forced a smile and said, "Welcome home, Oleander. We have heard quite a bit about you this past year. It's good to finally meet you."

"Thank you. Nice to meet you, too."

"Azura! Oleander!" a familiar voice called, cutting through the weird tension. Lorella and two younger girls were walking through the crowd. "Morning, girls! Oleander, I want you to meet a couple of my daughters, your cousins. This is Violet and Nessa."

I was relieved to have the distraction. "I'm so happy to meet you. I can't believe I have cousins." Violet seemed to be about my age, and Nessa a year or two younger. They were gorgeous. I was beginning to wonder if any faery was ugly.

The girls just stared at me, but didn't respond. I looked at Azura for help. They were obviously not pleased to meet me.

"Violet just turned seventeen. It's too bad you weren't able to grow up together. I'm sure you would have been great friends. But it's not too late." Azura smiled at Violet.

"Violet, why don't you take Oleander to meet some of your friends? I'll catch up with you in a moment," Azura said.

Violet rolled her eyes and stalked off. I followed

behind her, not sure what to make of her obvious disdain.

I should say something. Compliment her? It would be nice to have friends in this realm. "I like the way you have your hair," I said in an attempt to start a conversation. She had several braids of her honey-colored hair piled high on her head and large blue eyes. There was a sprinkle of freckles across the bridge of her nose.

She stared at me sideways, as if she was trying to figure out if I was making fun of her or not, but finally mumbled a "thanks" under her breath.

Humph. Heck with the nice routine. I stopped in my tracks. "Why are you acting like this? I haven't done anything to you and you barely know me."

Violet bit the side of her lip. I knew she couldn't lie. "I guess I'm sort of jealous. You've always been the special one, the precious daughter, the one everyone mourned the loss of. Suddenly, you're back in the picture and it takes you a year to visit us? What makes you so special that you can't even come home? And all everyone is talking about is how beautiful and powerful you are. Add to that, you're promised to the dark prince."

"You know of my promise to Kallan?" I asked, surprised.

"Of course, everyone knows. Half the girls here have a crush on him."

I couldn't help but laugh. I didn't know why I found that so funny. Who would have thought that light faeries would have crushes on dark ones? I thought it was taboo, but that probably added to the allure.

"Do dark and light faeries date?" I asked.

"Not often, but it does happen."

Interesting.

"I've heard that Kallan hasn't been involved with anyone since he met you. He used to go through girls like faeries go through faery dust."

"Faery dust is real?" I couldn't believe that Kallan wasn't dating anyone. For some reason, the thought made my pulse race.

Violet laughed. "No, it's not real. It's just a saying we use. Kinda like your human saying of raining cats and dogs. I've never been able to get that one. Humans have strange phrases."

"Oh." I grinned. "I guess we do. The other day I asked my mom why we say 'I feel sick as a dog.' She didn't know the answer."

"So what's he like? The dark prince?" Violet asked. "I've only seen him from afar a few times."

I smiled. "He's stubborn, moody, and has a temper, but he's also very thoughtful."

"You forgot how handsome he is." There was definitely a swoon-worthy note to her voice. "He sounds perfect. So why don't you want to marry him?"

"I have a boyfriend."

Violet scrunched up her nose. "A human?"

"Yes, a human," I retorted. "He's very sweet. We've been together for a long time."

Violet started walking again, so I tried to keep up. She walked as if she were floating on air, and I felt awkward next to her.

"Faeries belong with faeries," Violet told me, as if she couldn't believe that I could possibly be interested in a human.

It kind of ticked me off, but I didn't feel like arguing with her so I ignored the statement and turned to the less talkative Nessa. "So what do you do here for fun?"

"All sorts of things, I guess. We have parties,

dances, sports games, and stuff," she answered quietly before pushing her shoulder-length blonde hair behind a pointed ear.

"Sometimes we go to the human realm to hang out," Violet added.

"Really? We should do something together."

"That would be fun," Violet offered, her face softening. "I'm sorry I wasn't very welcoming. I dreaded meeting you."

"That's okay. I dreaded coming here."

"Why?"

"I don't know. I guess it makes all so real. It's a lot to take in."

"I can see that. I can't believe you went sixteen years without knowing you were a faery. It must have been quite a shock."

"That's an understatement." Relative or not, I barely knew the girl and wasn't ready to bare my soul, so I switched gears. "Do you have a boyfriend?"

"Not right now. I've got a couple of guys in my sights, but haven't done anything about it yet."

"Shouldn't be that hard to get whatever guy you want. You're gorgeous."

Her face reddened. "You don't have to say that."

"It's true." I watched some faeries go by. Many of them were staring and pointing at me.

"They'll get used to you. You're the most excitement we've had in a long time."

I felt like some freak show on display. My birthmark pulsed, ever-present and always pinpointing me as different.

"Oleander," Azura called.

We stopped and waited for her to catch up.

"Did you meet anyone new?"

"No. We were just catching up. I think Violet and I

are going to be great friends," I said, giving my cousin a genuine smile. We had a rocky start, but she was still my blood.

Violet's face glowed.

"See that group of children playing in the field?" Azura pointed at a group of about eight younger kids playing with a ball. None of them had wings yet, so they all had to be under sixteen.

"Yeah?"

"Those are your cousins, too."

"Wow. There are so many of them." I'd always been an only child. It was a shock to find out I had this many relatives.

"I'm going to go help my mother. I hope to see more of you before you go home," Violet said.

"Definitely." I waved as we walked off in opposite directions.

"I'd like to introduce you to someone else," Azura told me, motioning for me to follow.

"Who?"

She didn't say right away. She walked up to a group of faeries that were spreading out tablecloths. "Foster, Alva, this is Oleander."

They turned to face me. A sweet smile spread across the older woman's face. "It is so nice to meet you, Oleander. Do you know who I am?"

"No." I shook my head. How in the world was I supposed to know who she was?

"I am your Maimeó."

Confused, I looked at Azura. "What does that mean?"

"This is your other grandmother."

Maimeó looked older than Móraí, but not by much. Just like with Móraí, I had a hard time believing this woman was old enough to be my grandmother. She didn't have one wrinkle on her face. Her light brown hair was cut short, exposing the back of her neck.

"That would mean she's your husband's mom?" I asked Azura quietly.

"Yes. Your father's parents."

"And this is your Daideó, your grandfather," Maimeó said.

The older gentleman who stood next to her nodded at me. His blue eyes twinkled as he stepped forward and embraced me. "It is so good to finally hold you. Let me get a good look at you." He placed his strong hands on my shoulders and pulled back to look me over. He nodded, like he approved, then he ran his fingers over my birthmark. "An Aurorian," he said, as if he were confirming it to himself.

Maimeó spoke again, "This is my son, Durin, and my daughter, Marigold."

My family was growing larger by the second. There was no way I would keep all these names and faces straight. Durin and Marigold were about Azura's age, give or take. It was hard to tell how old anyone was here since they aged so slowly. They had light brown hair and blue eyes. One could definitely tell they were siblings.

"It's nice to meet you." I smiled, feeling like a parrot since I kept saying the same thing. Inside, I wasn't sure how I felt. I knew it wasn't their fault their son had been willing to trade me, but it still stung. What if it was the way he was raised? What if these family members were like him? What kind of person gave away their own child for power?

"You should have met us long ago," Maimeó said, turning to Azura. "I wish you had at least told us what you had done."

"I couldn't risk it," Azura replied.

"We're family. You could have trusted us."

"So was Oren and look what he did," Azura said tightly.

A look of shame crossed Maimeó's face. "I cannot excuse his actions. What he did was not right. We did not raise him that way."

"I know," Azura said softly. "We must go. We have a lot to do."

Thoughts—both good and bad—were flying around in my head. Obviously there was tension between my mother and these grandparents. I had so many questions to ask, but Azura was dragging me away. I wondered what my father looked like. Did he look like one of his parents? Or like his brother? Or something opposite?

Did I look like him?

CHAPTER TWELVE

When we got back to Azura's house, Lorella and Violet were placing food on a long wooden table in the front yard. I was dying to take a bite of the melon-type fruit, but nobody else was eating yet.

Azura handed me a large lime-green bowl filled with some sort of meat dish. I had no idea what it was, but it smelled delicious. "Would you put this on the table, please, Oleander?"

After the table was set, the children brought over flowers for decorations. One of the little girls walked up to me and tugged on my dress. "Will you play with us?"

"Sure, what do you want to play?"

"Bubbles."

"I love bubbles." I took her hand and she led me to the field. A teen with shimmering light green wings held a humongous bubble in her hand. She let it go and the bubble floated towards us. "What do we do?"

I asked.

"Catch it and get inside."

"Inside? Of the bubble?" I should have known the little faery meant something other than blowing bubbles.

"Of course!"

Very carefully, the girl caught the bubble. First, she put her hand in it, then her arm, and her leg. But as she put her head in, the bubble popped, spraying me with water. I laughed. "I'm not sure I'm talented enough to do that."

Another bubble floated our way. "You never know unless you try," an older girl told me.

She had me there. I opened my arms wide and gently caught the bubble. It felt like a delicate balloon. A soft breeze came along and the bubble wobbled. I almost lost it. I stuck my arms in, and then my head. I opened my mouth and made sure I could breathe. Cool! I thought to myself. As I tried to step in, the bubble popped.

"Oh!" a voice came from behind me.

I turned around. Standing a foot away were my two grandmothers, water dripping from them.

"Oops," I said sheepishly.

"It's a shame you did not grow up with Bubbles," Maimeó said, clucking her tongue.

Mórai flicked water off her fingertips with a laugh. "You could try over and over, Oleander. It gets harder to get inside that darn bubble every time!"

I laughed. "Is it even possible?"

Mórai nodded, her smile mischievous. "It sure is, but we're not going to tell you the secret, are we, Alva?"

Maimeó shook her head. "Takes all the fun out of it. But I do wish she'd been with us sooner. To grow up playing these games."

"As do I, Alva."

"She's here now, so let's all have a great time together." Azura stepped between us and took my hand. "Come, I want you to meet a friend."

She took me across the yard to a little man who stood by a tree. He couldn't have been taller than two feet and was dressed in brown.

"Hello!" he greeted me happily.

I noted his lack of wings, and without thinking, I asked, "What are you?"

"Oleander," Azura chided.

"No, it's fine," the little man said jovially. "She's never seen a dwarf before."

I could honestly say I hadn't. "Only in *Snow White.*"

The little guy laughed. "Well, I don't have six brothers, only two. We do go to work in the mines and find crystals for the faeries to cherish."

I began to wonder if every fantasy creature was real. "What's your name?"

"Dain."

"Well, it's nice to meet you, Dain."

A bell rang.

"It's time to eat." Azura clapped. "Oh, Oleander, you're in for such a treat."

"Do we sit somewhere in particular?"

"No. Wherever you want."

I grabbed a bowl and filled it with fruits, breads, and some of that meat dish I saw earlier. I looked around and plopped down underneath a tree. Without wasting another second, I took my first bite and closed my eyes with a groan. When I opened them again, I found Violet and Nessa had joined me.

"Warren keeps checking Oleander out," Nessa

said before taking a bite from a large apple-shaped fruit.

Violet laughed. "Typical."

"Too bad she's taken. They'd go well together."

"I am sitting right here," I interrupted, amused.

"Sorry." Nessa blushed.

"It's okay." I ate another bite of the fruit. "Which one is Warren?"

"The one with the auburn hair and red wings." Nessa pointed.

"Tell us about the human world," Violet said curiously.

"What do you want to know?"

"Everything."

"Uh..." I had no idea what to tell them. I started with school. They were amazed that I rode in cars every day. And they couldn't quite grasp the Internet or Facebook. To them, it seemed absurd not to just have a face-to-face conversation with someone.

After we finished eating, I jumped up to help clean up some of the bowls. I figured it was the least I could do since everyone was being so nice to me. Azura stopped me and said, "Watch."

A faery stood in front of the tables of empty dishes. She held her hands above her head and water rose out of the stream nearby. The arc of water splashed onto the dishes, swirling around bowls and plates, and then it drained from the table. The dishes were left clean and empty. Just by waving her hands, she'd manipulated the water to clean up.

"Let's go sit." Azura led me to a spot in the yard overlooking the stream. I sat quietly, letting the soft wind play with my hair and enjoying the sun on my face.

"Could I ever bring a friend here?" I asked.

"We don't usually let humans just come in and out."

"I understand...but she's my best friend. She'd love it here."

"This is the friend with the brown hair who picks you up for school?"

"Yeah, Sierra."

Azura smiled. "I've always liked her."

"She's the best."

"Is she the one you chose to confide in?"

I gaped at her, surprised. "How did you know?"

With a chuckle, Azura shrugged. "I know you have been struggling with things. I'm glad you have someone to talk to."

"You're not mad?"

"Of course not. I trust your judgment."

I took a deep breath and asked the question that had been niggling at me for almost a year. "What happens if I can't get out of the promise?"

"We'll deal with it."

"I don't want to be stuck in the dark world."

"No matter what, we'll make sure you aren't." She glanced at my necklace. "You like Kallan, don't you?"

I ran my fingers along the black stones. "Yeah. But I don't want to be with him because we have to."

"And Adam?"

I groaned. "I love him, too. I don't know what to do. It's really not fair."

She patted my hand. "We'll figure it out."

"How?"

"Your heart will tell you when the time is right."

I rolled my eyes. Why did everyone think I would just magically know? They had no idea what I was going through.

I was relieved when Violet's voice interrupted the conversation. "May I steal Oleander for a minute, Aunt Azura?"

"Of course." Azura smiled, obviously happy things were going well between us.

Violet tugged me in the direction of a group of guys. "They've been talking about you all day, about how much they wanted to meet you. I was sick of listening to them, so I figured I'd introduce you."

I smiled, not sure what to say.

Violet went around the circle, telling me their names, but other than the two normal names—Warren and Drake—the others were so strange I knew I couldn't spell them, much less remember what they were.

"So I hear you're promised to someone else?" a blond faery asked. His wings were mostly white, but had orange tips.

"Unfortunately." And even if I wasn't, I was still in love with Adam.

"That sucks."

"You're telling me."

The blond faery laughed. The five of them were definitely attractive, but none of them made me feel the way Kallan did.

We hung out with the guys for a couple of hours. It didn't take long for me to realize that Violet had a crush on the blond faery. He seemed to be interested in her, too. I remembered my attempt at matchmaking with Sierra and decided I would stay out of it.

Azura came up and softly asked, "Would you come with me, Oleander?"

I waved to Violet and her friends, then followed Azura to a large clearing behind the row of houses where Azura lived. The sky turned darker as the sun got closer to the horizon. I was almost sad to find the day was over. The light faery world seemed like such a happy place. If I did have to marry Kallan, we'd have to talk about where to live. Living in that castle he called home seemed like a lifetime of punishment to me.

A few older faeries were throwing wood in the middle of the open field. The growing pile was surrounded by large stones.

"What's going on?" I asked, looking to Azura for clarification.

She gestured to a stout, flame-haired faery who put his hands over the wood and closed his eyes. "The bonfire is the end of the celebration," Azura whispered.

Beneath the faery's hands, the woodpile burst into flames. In seconds, the wood was engulfed, and flickering orange flames reached high into the sky.

Suddenly, fireworks exploded above us. Wide-eyed, I took Azura's warm hand in mine, and we leaned on each other, our gazes on the sky.

I realized I could get used to living in a place like this, and that scared me.

CHAPTER
THIRTEEN

Sunday morning, I was back home and studying at my desk just like Azura had promised. My mind kept floating back to the faery world, and then to Kallan, and then Adam. I'd texted both Sierra and Adam early on telling them I had a lot of homework to do and would talk to them later that night. Then I turned my cell phone off and forced myself to focus on my schoolwork. I was glad my parents didn't pester me about the time I spent away. It must have been killing them. I just wasn't ready to talk about it yet.

Halfway through my science homework, I turned my phone on. My heart sank when I saw there wasn't a text from Kallan. Two days had passed and he hadn't replied to the text I sent. I wondered if he went home for the spring equinox and that's why I hadn't heard from him. That was probably the case. But why didn't he let me know he was leaving? Not like he had to answer to me or anything. Or maybe he was mad at me over what happened the last time we were together. I sighed and tossed the phone on the bed to stop myself from checking it every few moments.

I was so immersed in my schoolwork, the sharp rap on my door startled me. Mom called, "Rylie, come eat."

"Be right out." I dropped my pencil, grateful for the distraction. Throwing my arms in the air, I stretched. I felt like my eyes were going to cross from all the studying.

My parents sat at the dining room table with a large box of pizza in front of them. My mouth watered at the fresh, garlicky smell that filled the room.

My mom smiled warmly. "Thought you could use a break."

"I'm starving." I took the chair next to her, and my dad handed me a plastic plate with a couple of slices of pizza.

"How's the homework going?" Mom asked.

I groaned. "It's never ending. I don't know how I'll ever catch up."

"One thing at a time," Dad spoke up. "If you need any help, let us know."

"Thanks, Dad."

"So are you going to tell us about the faery world or keep us in suspense?" Mom asked, her brown eyes dancing with excitement. I still found it hard to believe that my mom thought it was cool I was a faery.

Between mouthfuls of pizza, I gave them the scoop on my weekend with Azura. They asked questions and seemed really interested, which felt so weird.

Later that evening, I was brushing my teeth getting ready for bed when my phone dinged. I rinsed quickly and hurried to my phone sitting on the edge of the desk. I smiled when I saw the name that scrolled across the screen. Kallan.

Sorry I didn't reply. I had to go home. There is something I need to talk to you about. In person.

My heart beat a little faster. *Um, Ok.*

I'll meet you outside your house again.

I glanced at the clock—it was just after eleven. *Now?*

Give me 5 minutes.

I tugged on a sweatshirt and stepped into my tennis shoes, taking my time. I wondered what was so important he needed to talk to me now, and sincerely hoped it wasn't bad news.

In the dark back yard, Kallan's wings glowed. I ran towards him, my heart rate going out of control. The way he made me feel, I sometimes believed I could walk away from my life and start a new one with him. The feeling was even stronger after my weekend with Azura.

I stopped short when I saw how serious his face was.

Panic rose in my chest. "What is it? You're not taking me back now, are you?"

He shook his head. "No. That's not it."

"What is it then?" I snapped.

"It's about your dad," he said quietly.

"My dad? Has something happened?" I thought he was in bed sleeping.

"Not your human father, Rylie. Your biological father."

"Oh!" I relaxed. "What about him?"

"There's been a sighting."

I inhaled sharply. "He's alive?"

"It seems so. My father has been searching for

him since you surfaced."

"Why?"

"If he's alive, my father has to hold up his end of the bargain."

"I don't understand."

Kallan shifted his weight to his other foot. "If Oren knows you're alive, and that the deal can be completed, he might come after you."

"But Varwik and I already have a deal."

"True. However, I still worry. I was hoping Oren was dead. It bothers me that he hasn't come to collect. It's like he's waiting for something. He must have heard by now that you're alive. It's been almost a year. Our world is small and news travels fast. So what is he waiting for?"

I shrugged. "Maybe he just enjoys his new life and doesn't want to get caught up with any of this anymore. He's brought shame to his family. You should've seen the looks on his parents' faces when I met them."

Kallan rubbed his brow. "We really thought he was dead. My father has men scouring both the faery and human realms looking for him. He's been evading them until recently. Someone saw him in the human realm."

"He's here?" I gasped. "He's been living with humans all this time?"

"It seems so." Kallan shook his head. "I don't like this at all."

"I can't believe he's alive."

"If he's alive, then my father is obligated to complete the deal."

"And?"

Kallan clenched his jaw. "If Oren doesn't come to collect, my father will be furious. I think he might take it out on you. I'm...scared that he could hurt you."

I rolled my eyes. "Your father is a brute and bully."

Kallan chuckled. "That he is. I'm sure once your father is caught, the deal will remain. It's just very odd that he is avoiding us."

"From what I know of him, you'd think he'd be jumping at the chance to have this magick."

Kallan was silent for a moment, and then he stepped forward. The movement put him in my personal space, and my breath caught in my throat. He brushed his fingers down my face. "If he tries to talk to you, promise you'll let me know."

I backed away, my hands coming up like mini shields between us. "I don't like making promises anymore."

He rolled his eyes. "Just let me know."

"Do you think he will? I don't even know what he looks like."

"I don't know. I just want to protect you from any further pain." Kallan's eyes met mine briefly before he looked away into the dark woods. The man who bargained my life for his gain could be alive—could come back. My mind raced with all the implications. It was too much to take in.

Kallan cleared his throat. "I heard you went to the spring equinox festival. What did you think?"

"You heard?" I asked suspiciously.

He flashed me an arrogant grin. "We have ears everywhere. It seems quite a few of the boys are smitten with you. Not that I blame them."

There was a slight growl in his voice that gave me goose bumps. "You're one to talk. The girls I met were all in a flurry that I'm promised to the dark prince. They wanted to hear all about you. I was pretty surprised to learn that the light and dark interact sometimes."

Kallan shrugged. "It's not unheard of." He paused. "Have you ever considered that maybe you are meant to bring faeries together instead of tear us apart?"

I stared at him. "What do you mean?"

"Aurorian faeries are so rare and powerful. The last one tore us apart. Perhaps you are meant to bring us together."

I had never thought of it that way. Talk about holding the weight of the world on your shoulders. It did sound a lot better than destroying each other. I still wasn't ready to resign to my fate. If there was a way out of the promise, I was going to take it. I had no doubt about that.

"I should get you back home. I didn't want you to hear about your father from anyone else. I also want you to be prepared in case he shows up on your door-step."

"Thank you. I should probably talk to Azura."

Kallan nodded.

Once I was safely back in my house. I changed into my pajamas and crawled into bed, where I stared at the ceiling with my mind whirling. My father was alive, but had never sought contact with me. A year after my existence had come to light, he had suddenly been "sighted." What was he up to? Other than trying to find a way to use this to his advantage, I thought, disgusted. Why wouldn't he want dark magick? Unless he had changed. But how would I know that unless I met him?

And unfortunately, I wasn't sure that I wanted to meet him.

CHAPTER FOURTEEN

Adam greeted me on the front steps the next morning with a long kiss. "I've missed you," he murmured, brushing his hands through my hair. "I know it's only been two days, but it feels much longer."

"I've missed you, too. I'm sorry I've been so busy lately." Guilt filled me when I thought of seeing Kallan last night. I was keeping so much from Adam.

"We've both been busy. Baseball takes up a lot of my time."

And faeries take up a lot of mine, I thought wryly. "So what did you do last night?"

Adam grabbed my backpack and slung it on his other shoulder. "Went out with the guys to celebrate my acceptance into Southern California. We had a blast."

Usually Adam would have invited me to go out with him. I should have been there with him to celebrate, but instead I was stuck doing homework. And having clandestine meetings with a guy I was supposed to marry. What kind of girlfriend was I? A horrible one, that's what. I tried to push the negative thoughts aside, for now.

"We're going to the spring fling dance, right?" I squeezed his hand and smiled up at him, hoping he couldn't tell that a dance was the last thing on my mind.

"Of course. It's this Friday, right?"

"What tipped you off? The thousand posters plastered around the school?"

Adam laughed. "The guys are complaining they don't want to go, but they always cave."

Adam pushed open the door and almost banged into Kallan.

"Adam," Kallan said curtly.

"Kallan."

The door shut behind the dark faery, and I turned to Adam. "You know him?"

Adam's jaw clenched. "I know him. He's trying to take my place as pitcher. Coach has made him the backup."

"Oh." I wasn't sure how to respond. "Is he any good?"

"Real good. He seems like a prick, if you ask me."

I inhaled sharply. Adam rarely used language like that. "Why would you say that? You hardly know him."

He shot me a crazed look. "He just waltzed out onto the field and told the coach he wanted to take over as starting pitcher."

My lip twitched. I could see Kallan doing that. "Yeah, that does sound a little arrogant. What did the coach do?"

"He tossed him the ball, and then the jerk struck

out five of our best hitters."

That didn't sound good. I wondered if Kallan used his power to influence the coach and to play well. Just the thought made me furious. Baseball was everything to Adam. There was no way I was going to let Kallan take that from him, especially since he was trying to take me too.

I gripped Adam's hand tighter. "I'm sure you have nothing to worry about. You hold every record in this school."

Adam stopped in front of my locker, his face still tense. "For now," he muttered under his breath.

Great. Just what I needed. Two alpha males going at each other. I had to talk to Kallan soon to squash this before it went any further.

Later that afternoon when I was in the library doing research, Kallan walked by my table, his nose in a book. My wings fluttered and the blood rushed to my face. I hated the way my body reacted to him.

Closing my notebook, I stood up and followed him down the aisle. Thankfully, the library was relatively quiet other than a few freshmen studying.

"Kallan," I whispered.

He turned, his book snapping shut. "I'm surprised you're talking to me in public."

"Why are you messing with Adam?" I hissed.

Kallan met my eyes. "I don't leave things up to chance."

"What does that mean?"

"I didn't come here to watch you run around with your boyfriend. I came here to win your love."

I took a step back, surprised by his words. "Then do it fairly. Please, Kallan. Just leave him out of it."

"It means that much to you?"

I stared at the inky black hair that fell over his eye and had to stop myself from brushing it out of the way. "Yes. It really does. It's not his fault. Can't you just play another position or something? Baseball is really important to him. More important than anything."

Kallan raised an eyebrow. "More important than you?"

"Don't be ridiculous." I glared at him. "You're not going to win any points with me by doing this. In fact, that would do the opposite. If my love is really what you are after, I suggest you reconsider." I spun on my heel and hurried out of the library. Once I was in the hall, I realized I left my books inside. "Damn it."

Before I could turn around and go back through the swinging door, Kallan emerged. I recognized the sparkly purple folder under the stack of books he held, and it made me even angrier that he was being such a gentleman.

He offered them to me, his face unreadable. "You forgot something."

"Thanks."

"I'm sorry. I didn't realize it would bother you so much. I was just sick of hearing how great he is. My competitive streak came out."

I moved the books to my other hip and studied his face. "Really?"

"I'll talk to the coach. I'd rather play first base. Maybe he'll give me that slot. The guy they have now is terrible."

I sighed and felt the tension leave my body. "Thank you."

The rest of the week passed quickly. Between music rehearsals, trying to catch up with my homework, and taking tests, I barely had any free time. When Friday arrived, I couldn't believe I forgot to go shopping for a dress.

I pictured all the dresses that were at Azura's house. Any one of them would be perfect. Too bad her house wasn't closer. I looked in my closet with disgust. Nothing would do. Everything was old. I needed a new dress.

I couldn't believe I was doing it, but I picked up my phone and called Azura. She must have been in our realm, because she picked up on the second ring.

"Hey, I hate to bother you, but I have a dance tonight and nothing to wear."

"Say no more. I know the perfect dress. I'll be there shortly." The excitement was evident in her voice.

I felt a little guilty enlisting Azura's help, so I yelled down the stairs for my mom.

She came up the stairs a minute later. "What's wrong, sweetie?"

"There's a dance tonight."

"Oh, how neat!" Mom beamed.

"I want my hair to be curly. Can you do it?"

"Can I? Rylie, I'd love to!"

I sat down at my desk and handed her the curling iron. "Azura is bringing me a dress."

"Oh." Mom's face fell.

"I didn't have anything to wear and she has a lot of dresses for me at her place," I rushed to explain.

"I see. Well, it's a great idea. She obviously has good taste. Let's get busy on your hair."

I could tell that it bothered her, and it made me feel horrible. It wasn't easy trying to please everyone.

Just as Mom pulled the curling iron down and the

last curl sprang into place, the doorbell rang.

"That must be Azura. I'll go let her in. You look amazing, sweetie." My mom smiled and slipped out the door.

A few moments later, Azura glided into the room with a garment bag draped on her forearm. She pulled out a simple, sage-green chiffon dress. I grabbed it from her and shooed both her and my mother out of the bathroom.

I tossed off my clothes and stepped into the dress. It had spaghetti straps and a sweetheart neckline. Three off-white ribbons wrapped just under my chest and the bottom was gauzy and flowed when I walked. It was breathtaking. It looked like something a Greek goddess would wear. My mother was right; Azura had great taste. I spun around and stared at myself in the full-length mirror. The color even complemented my wings.

"Let us see," my mom called.

I pushed the door open and walked into my bedroom. Both of my mothers covered their mouths. They stood oohing and ahhing over me like I was a princess or something. The attention was nice, and I had to admit, I was glad they were both there.

I twirled around the room and curtsied. "I love the dress. Thank you."

"You're welcome. Your mother and I were just saying how beautiful you are." Azura grinned proudly.

I was surprised to hear her say "your mother." I smiled back. "I'm pretty lucky to have two mothers."

Azura had tears in her eyes, and my mom was beaming. Maybe this really could work out after all.

"Do I look okay?" I asked.

"Perfect," Azura replied.

"I'd love to see how you really look," Mom hinted.

I smiled nervously. "Really?"

She nodded. "Please."

I dropped the glamour and allowed my mother to see me as a faery. Her face lit up. "You are so lovely! I wish the world could see you like this."

"The world would freak out, Mom."

The doorbell rang, and I heard Dad answer it. "Hey, Adam, come on in."

"I'll be down in a minute," I called. I put the glamour back on, glanced in the mirror one more time, and with a final smile at my moms, I walked down the stairs.

Adam grinned as I came into view. "You look beautiful."

"I'll second that," Dad said. "You'll be the most beautiful girl at the dance."

"Oh, stop." I rolled my eyes and laced my arm through Adam's. "Shall we?"

I kissed my parents goodbye and thanked Azura again. I wasn't quite ready to hug or kiss her yet.

Adam swung open the door and led me out. After we were both in the car, he turned to me. "That lady has been here a lot lately."

"Yeah."

He started the truck. "So who exactly is she?"

My heart pounded. How was I supposed to answer this question without lying? "I don't want to talk about it."

He glanced over at me. "What?"

"It's a long story, and I just don't want to get into it right now."

"You know you can tell me anything."

Right. I was sure if I told him I was a freaking faery, he'd be cool with it and we'd go to the dance like nothing happened. "I know. I'd really like to just go to the dance and forget about my family for a while."

His jaw clenched, and he stared at me for a minute before answering. "Fine."

I could tell his feelings were hurt, but I had no idea how to tell him about Azura without spilling the whole truth. Maybe I should tell him that I was switched at birth, and Azura was my birth mother. That was the truth. It just left out the faery part. But I didn't feel ready and certainly didn't want to do it before a dance. It was just too much to deal with.

CHAPTER FIFTEEN

When we pulled up to the school, Adam turned to me like he had more to say, but I stopped him before he even started. I tilted my head and smiled at him. "Please, let's just have a good time tonight. I'll tell you about it some other time."

His face softened. "Okay." He opened his door, hurried around the side of the truck, and extended his hand for me to get down. Hand in hand, we walked into school.

The theme was secret gardens, and they did a wonderful job. Of course, it didn't come close to the faery world, but they tried.

We walked over a small white wooden bridge into the gymnasium, which was filled with colorful balloons, fake clouds, cardboard trees, and brightly colored paper flowers. The lights were dim and a flashing beam made its way around the large room. The dance floor was almost empty, but it was early.

To the left, people were lining up to get their photographs taken. I pulled Adam over to the line. I'd never hear the end of it from my parents if I didn't get my photo taken. I also loved seeing myself in my human form, and a photo was the only way I still could. I used to be camera shy, but since becoming a full-fledged faery, I allowed myself to be photographed whenever the chance allowed. It was a way to document myself as a human girl without the wings and promises.

We stood in front of the cloud background and smiled when the cameraman pulled out a stuffed monkey from his back—even though we knew it was coming after watching couples that went before us.

Laughing, we made our way towards the refreshments. I caught sight of Sierra and she beckoned to us.

"Over here!"

When we joined her, she introduced us to her date, Brett. He was from one of the neighboring schools. I laughed to myself. She went from Ian, who was considered "goth" with his dyed black hair and piercings, to a blond-haired, blue-eyed "All-American" boy.

The four of us walked over to get a glass of punch. A large DJ booth had been set up next to the stand. One of Sierra's favorite songs came on, and she pulled us out onto the dance floor. The music pulsed through my body. I swayed to the rhythm and grinned up at Adam. He wasn't much of a dancer, but he always humored me anyway. Glitter covered the floors and the strobe lights made it look like a field of diamonds. The song came to an end and a slow tune filled the air.

Adam took me in his arms and I pressed my body to his. Resting my head on his chest, I listened to the steady beat of his heart. As the song came to an end, I looked up into Adam's eyes and felt comfort and love. Our lips met and I closed my eyes. It felt right being with Adam. We were so comfortable together. We broke apart and out of the corner of my eye, I saw sparkly teal wings pushed back against the wall, trying not to be seen.

Kallan. He was watching me.

"Bathroom break!" I announced loudly, grabbing Sierra.

Adam raised an eyebrow but didn't protest.

I pulled Sierra to the bathroom, and as soon as the door cut off the music, I groaned. "Kallan's here."

"So? He goes to school with us, you know. Pretty much everyone is here."

My shoulders slumped. She was right, of course. He was allowed to be here, and I was overreacting. Making a big deal out of nothing. "He's watching me."

"From what you've told me, he's in love with you, so yeah, he probably is." She handed me her lip-gloss. I didn't really need it, but put it on anyway.

"This is all so confusing."

"What? Having two guys in love with you?" She sounded a bit annoyed.

"Yes. You try it," I snapped.

"I wouldn't mind. Look at Brett. Easy on the eyes, but boring as hell."

I couldn't help but laugh.

She smiled. "Let's get back out there. Did you see Ian is here with Morgan?"

"Really? She doesn't seem his type." I pushed the bathroom door open. The music was so loud I could feel it vibrate throughout my chest.

Adam was talking to his buddies. I stood by his side and waited for him to finish. I scanned the room for Kallan, but didn't see him anywhere. Adam put his arm around me, and we chatted with the group for a few minutes.

"Can I steal you away for another dance?" I whispered to him as a slow song began.

He grinned. "Anytime."

We rocked back and forth on the dance floor. I was trying to forget seeing Kallan and focus on my perfect boyfriend, but suddenly, Kallan was there.

He tapped Adam on the shoulder. "May I cut in?"

Adam's expression went from shock to anger. "No. You may not."

There was a beat, and then Kallan growled, "Shouldn't you give her a chance to answer?"

Adam stood rooted to the spot, holding me firm. "I don't know what kind of game you're playing, but it's not going to work. Rylie is mine."

Kallan stared at me, eyebrow raised. "You can't speak for yourself?"

"I-I'm with Adam," I said, looking away as my cheeks flamed.

People had started to notice the confrontation. Couples around us stopped dancing to stare. I met Kallan's eyes and sent him a look. For a moment, I wished I could talk to him in my mind. I debated using his power and making him go elsewhere, but I couldn't do that him. Once had been enough. I knew he wouldn't do it to me.

Kallan must have understood my look, and he backed off. "Fair enough."

Adam steered me away. "Can you believe that guy? Asking my girl to dance?"

This was not going to end well. Whatever happened...whatever my decision...it was going to destroy someone.

Later that evening, I lay in bed stuck in thoughts of Adam, Kallan, and what would happen if it came down to a fight. I shoved my face in the pillow, when I heard something hit the window. At first I thought I had imagined it until it happened twice more. I threw the blankets off and tentatively pushed the curtain to the side.

Kallan was standing outside my window. What was he doing here at this time of night? He'd lost his mind. Why couldn't he be normal and call?

I held my finger up signaling one minute. I looked down at my purple plaid PJ pants and white cami. I should change, but I was lazy, so I grabbed a sweatshirt, made myself invisible, and hurried outside.

"Did I wake you?" Kallan asked.

"No, I couldn't sleep," I said honestly. "Too much on my mind. What's so important you had to come? Haven't you done enough tonight?" I took a few deep breaths to keep calm and not blow up at him.

"I'm sorry about the dance."

"Kallan, you have to stop that. Adam was pissed."

"I wasn't too thrilled myself. So what? You're not allowed to dance with anyone else? That's pretty lame. I didn't take you for the submissive type."

"I'm not. I just didn't want to stir things up. Things are bad enough as they are." We walked towards the woods. "Why are you here?"

Kallan stopped and turned toward me. "You owe me a dance."

"Are you serious? You came out here to dance with me?"

"You say that like you're surprised. Let me tell you how it was for me. All night I had to watch the girl I love in someone else's arms. The whole time wishing it were my arms you were in."

I looked down at the ground and then back into his eyes. They glistened in the moonlight. He was right.

Before I could talk myself out of it, I closed the space between us and wrapped my arms around his neck. His arms encircled my waist, his warm palms settling comfortably on my lower back as he tugged me close. My heart felt like it might jump out of my chest. I knew it was wrong, but I couldn't stop myself.

With my body pressed to his, there was no need for music. We moved together like we were floating on air. When I was with Kallan, it was as if the rest of the world didn't exist. I finally understood what living in the moment meant. I couldn't imagine being anywhere else.

"What were you thinking about when I came to your window?" Kallan asked softly.

I readjusted an arm, my hand resting on his strong shoulder. It wasn't like I could tell him I'd been imagining worst-case scenarios of a showdown between him and my boyfriend, so I opted for the other thing that had been on my mind lately. "I think I want to try and find my biological father. Before he finds me. I..." I trailed off, trying to think of the best way to voice my feelings. "I think I need to understand why he was willing to give me up and not collect what was owed."

I could feel his body tense. "I don't know if that is such a great idea. If my father can't find him, what makes you think you could?"

I shrugged, the movement somehow pulling him even closer. His thumbs brushed over my sweatshirt hypnotically. "I feel like I should at least try. I have so many unanswered questions."

"Then I'll go with you."

I smiled. "I'm not asking you to go with me. I just wanted to know what you thought of the idea."

"I don't like it. You don't know your way around the faery world."

"I thought you said he was in the human world."

"I did. But to find him, you'd probably have to go through the faery world."

"I'll figure it out. I'm an Aurorian, remember? I have tools at my disposal."

"Rylie! Stop being so obstinate and let me help you. I'd like to."

"Okay." I laughed. How had he lowered my guard? I felt easy and free dancing in his arms beneath the moonlight, no music, no worries. "If you want to come, then come. I'd like the company."

His arms tightened around me. "When do you want to leave?"

"Well, we just started spring break, so as soon as possible."

"Can you be ready by six?"

"A.M.?" I gawked at him.

His eyes sparkled. "Yes. Six in the morning."

I groaned. That was earlier than I had to get up for school. "If I have to."

"I'll pick you up then. What are you going to tell your parents?"

I bit the side of my lip. I wasn't sure whether or not I should tell my parents. I could either tell them and introduce them to Kallan, or I could just leave a note. They'd be upset either way. I had to figure out which one would be less upsetting. If I told them beforehand, they could try and stop me from going. Asking forgiveness is easier than asking for permission. But I didn't like being secretive with them. Especially when I didn't know how long I'd be gone. "I'm not sure.

Do you think we can check in enough for them not to notice I'm gone?"

"I doubt it. You should tell them something. Of course, we have the advantage of time difference if we go to the faery realm."

He was right. I couldn't let them worry that something bad had happened to me. "I should get some sleep. Since we're leaving so early."

"Thanks for letting me come with you," Kallan murmured. He was so close, I thought he was going to kiss me. I could feel his breath on my lips, a sudden tension in his shoulders. His sweet scent was intoxicating.

I closed my eyes, equal parts of me wanting him to do it and begging for him not to. I didn't think I could say no or stop it.

Instead, he let me go. When his arms left my body, I suddenly felt empty and alone. I was surprised to feel a twinge of disappointment.

"Thanks for the dance." He squeezed my hand, and then turned and loped away.

I went back inside, my skin still tingling and my heart fluttering in my chest. I chided myself for even hoping for a kiss. This wasn't like me at all.

How could he have such an effect on me? And what did that mean about my relationship with Adam?

CHAPTER SIXTEEN

"Way too early," I muttered to myself, shutting off my alarm at five in the morning. I had showered the night before so I only had to get dressed and brush my hair. I had no idea what to pack, so I grabbed a small backpack out of the closet and stuffed a couple outfits and a brush inside.

Trying not to make a sound, I tiptoed down the stairs. My footsteps silent on the plush carpet, I cut up the hallway and into the dark kitchen. Dad had already left for the day, and Mom was still fast asleep. She always slept in on the weekend. I couldn't leave without telling them something. They would be so worried. Especially after my last disappearance.

I looked at my watch and hurried over to the counter. I grabbed a pen and scribbled a quick note.

"Please don't worry. I'm going to search for my biological father. I need some answers. I might have to go to the faery world, but I shouldn't be gone too long in human time. If it takes longer than I expect I'll find a way to call. Love, Rylie"

I grabbed a magnet and stuck the note to the fridge. Closing my eyes, I took a deep breath and headed towards the front door.

I stepped outside and saw Kallan waiting for me by the trees. I hoped he wasn't coming with me for a different agenda. He didn't seem crazy about the idea. Maybe he really did just want to make sure I was safe.

I needed to trust him. I forced a smile and hurried over to where he was standing. I yawned. I should have grabbed a cup of coffee on the way out. "Here's something you should know about me," I said wryly.

"What's that?" He cocked his head to the side and studied me.

"I'm not a morning person."

He laughed. "I'll keep that in mind."

"So where are we going?" I asked as we walked into the forest. I glanced back over my shoulder at my house. Soon my mom would be awake and panicked. I wished there was another way, but this was something I had to do and asking for permission was a risk I couldn't take.

"We need to find the faery that said he saw Oren," Kallan said.

"Where's he?"

"He's a wanderer. Doesn't call anywhere home, so finding him may...be difficult."

"Great," I said sarcastically. "Do we at least have a starting place?"

"Yes." Kallan grinned. "Have some faith in me. I'm not going to take you on a wild goose chase. At least, not on purpose."

I did have faith in him, but I wasn't going to tell him that. We walked into the woods in silence. There was so much I wanted to say, wanted to know, but I felt that getting closer to Kallan was cheating on Adam. I knew I couldn't last long without talking, so I chose something safe to talk about. "How do you like school?"

"It's different. So much indoor learning, homework, and testing. I don't know how you do it."

"Faery schools are that different?"

"Yes. We do a lot of our learning outside. I've never had homework and the tests aren't written tests. We're taught with a more hands-on approach. When we're tested, it's more show than tell."

"What do you learn? I mean, do you learn more than how to use your powers? Do things with nature? Or is there more?"

He laughed. "Of course we learn other things. Math, geography, even science. It's not that the subject matter is different than what your schools teach, it's the way we're taught."

I wondered if I decided to live in the fey world, if I'd be required to go to their school. "Do your friends know about me?"

"Of course."

"What do they think?"

"They think you're hot." He stepped over a log and I followed.

I laughed. "That's not what I was asking."

"They don't know what to think. Our...situation is different. They think I've gone off the deep end coming to school here." He smiled.

"I don't blame them. It's pretty crazy." I paused. "Sierra knows."

"What? She knows everything?"

"I told her. I had to tell someone. I couldn't talk to my parents about...us."

He raised his eyebrows. "You talk about us?"

"Sometimes."

"What does she say?"

"Well, she doesn't understand the significance of the promises. She's my best friend and she's supportive. She thinks you're gorgeous, but she's known Adam as long as I have."

"What are you going to do, Rylie?"

I thought about Adam and how much I didn't want to hurt him. I also couldn't deny my feelings for Kallan. "I don't know." I pushed a branch out of the way. "Can we not talk about this right now? I just want to focus on finding Oren."

"Sure."

As we continued walking, the forest changed around us. The trees became taller, and fruit-covered bushes lined the floor. It didn't look as colorful and beautiful as the light faery land where Azura took me, but it wasn't dark faery land either, which meant we were in the neutral zone.

I was hungry. We had been walking for hours, and I forgot to eat breakfast. "When's lunch?"

Kallan chuckled. "Any time you want. All you have to do is say the word. Can't have you withering away."

"Then I choose now."

Kallan took my hand and pulled me behind a tree. He picked a few delicious-looking fruits off nearby bushes and handed me one. Biting into it was like tasting a piece of heaven. I closed my eyes in pleasure and enjoyed it to the very last bite.

Kallan dropped his backpack to the ground and pulled out a package of beef jerky. "You'll need protein. We could be out here for a while."

I shoved my hand in the bag, extracted a few pieces, and leaned against the tree. The jerky had a sweet maple taste to it, but I didn't like how hard I had to chew. I tried to focus on my surroundings. It was so relaxing in the woods. Birds chirped, and the soft breeze tickled my skin.

Kallan smiled as he handed me a bottle of water. "We should probably keep moving."

I helped myself to the cold, refreshing liquid and fell into step beside him. A short time later, a rustling sound from the bushes beside me broke through the forest sounds. I grabbed Kallan's arm. "What was that?"

He stared into the brush, going quiet for a few seconds, then answered, "Just keep walking."

I did as he instructed even though a creepy feeling lingered. My grip on his arm got tighter as the sound followed us.

Suddenly, an ugly creature jumped out in front of us. It was small and brownish and had a long, curved nose. The way his dark beady eyes looked at me made the hair on my arms stand up. I froze and my nails dug into Kallan's skin.

Kallan and the thing stared at each other. "What do you want, goblin?"

"Your father requests your presence."

Kallan's face was stoic. "I don't care. I'm busy."

"He sent me to escort you."

"Tell him I am not coming."

The goblin took an awkward step back. "But Prince, your father insisted."

"I'm. Not. Going." Kallan said each word very slowly. With that, he grabbed my hand and pulled me away. He looked back a few times, but the goblin didn't follow us. Finally his face softened and the worry lines disappeared.

"What was that all about?"

Kallan ran his hand through his hair. "My father wasn't happy with my decision to visit the human realm for so long, and he definitely doesn't like me helping you."

"I thought he wanted to find Oren."

"He does. On his own terms."

I swallowed hard. "What's going to happen now?"

"I don't know. He could send guards to force me back home or he could let it go for now."

"I don't see your father letting anything go." Varwik's face flashed before my eyes. I shuddered and pushed it out of my mind. "What exactly is a goblin?"

"Not a very nice creature. They're mischievous and can be evil. You don't want to be near them if they're hungry."

I didn't like the sound of that. "Where do they live?"

"They hide in the neutral lands. But my father will feed some of them if they do things for him." He shifted an arm around my shoulders and squeezed me playfully. "If it makes you cling to me like this, maybe I should have them stick around."

I slapped him in the arm. "Knock it off."

He tilted his head back and laughed.

CHAPTER SEVENTEEN

The sun was in the west when we came to a dark, denser area of the forest.

"Stay close," Kallan said, holding out a hand to indicate I should stay behind him.

"Why?" My voice was shaky.

"We call this Targore. There are a lot of...creatures here."

"Dangerous ones?"

"They can be."

"Maybe we should go a different way?"

"There isn't one. As long as you stay with me, you'll be safe."

I blew out a long breath. I did not consider myself a brave person, but I did feel slightly safer with him by my side. Not by much.

Kallan's blue-green gaze caught mine. "Are you sure you want to do this?"

Although I had a few doubts in my mind, I knew I wanted answers. And if this was the only way to get them... "Yes. I have to."

"You're stronger than you realize. You just need to embrace your power."

I wished it were that easy. We pushed forward, pine needles crunching below our feet. At least they looked like pine needles, except for the fact they were dark red instead of the green I was used to.

A huge creature at least seven feet tall stepped out in front of us. I froze. He looked half human and half reptile. A leather vest covered his chest and large knives were tethered at his side.

Kallan tensed under my grasp.

"You shouldn't be here," the monster growled.

"We're just passing through. Not here to cause any trouble," Kallan said with an edge to his voice.

The creature drew a sword from his hip.

"You shouldn't have done that," Kallan said calmly.

"Oh, really? And who are you to stop me? I can slice up you and your pretty girlfriend and feed you to the goblins."

Kallan's eyes glowed. He stared at the monster with an unwavering gaze. The monster fell to his knees, his eyes pleading, but not a word escaped his mouth.

"Let's go." Kallan stepped around the monster.

"What did you do to him?"

"What I had to. He gave me no choice." His mouth was set in a tight line. "I wiped his mind clean. He's as useless as a newborn baby now."

I inhaled sharply. "Couldn't you have just told him to let us pass?"

"No. He's a hunter. It's in his blood. He wouldn't

have let us go with a simple mind trick. He would have kept after us until we were both chopped into little pieces."

I shuddered. "I'm glad you're with me."

His eyes widened. "You don't think I'm a monster?"

"I would have been dead without you. I know it's not easy for you to use your gift to harm others."

Kallan didn't say anything, but I could see the tension leave his shoulders, and he relaxed as we trudged on.

I don't know how much time passed before Kallan stopped abruptly. "We're close. I need you to stay here for a moment. I need to talk to someone, and they won't talk to me if you're with me."

Panic rose in my chest. "No. You can't leave me out here. Kallan, please don't."

"I have to. Use your glamour and make yourself invisible. Stay here. I won't be far, so if anyone bothers you, use my power."

I nodded and tried to hold back the tears. I was terrified to be left alone.

"Stay here, Rylie. I'll be right back," Kallan repeated before slinking off.

As soon as he was gone, the forest seemed to close in. The darkness grew thick, and it was so quiet I could hear myself breathing. I gulped and tried to remain calm. Be brave, I told myself. I wrapped my arms around my torso, trying to fend off the chill. No one can see you. I tried to relax and be one with nature like a faery might be, but it wasn't helping.

The hoot of an owl made me jump. My eyes searched the trees and sky, looking for the source, but I didn't see anything. That didn't make me feel any better. Only a small amount of sun shone through the trees. It felt like the middle of the night where I stood.

What was taking Kallan so long? I wandered off in the direction he'd disappeared. I couldn't stand staying in one place. I had to keep reminding myself that no one could see me, and I was safe.

Time passed. It was probably just a few minutes, but it felt like hours. I realized I had wandered too far and had no idea where I was or which way to head. The forest looked the same every direction I looked. Trees, bushes, all the same. No way out.

I remembered what Azura had told me. I closed my eyes and took deep breaths. I stood completely still and tried to tune into the forest. I didn't feel the warmth or familiarity I did when I had been with Azura. But I did feel something. Coldness and danger behind me, but not to the left. The left was more... friendly.

I opened my eyes, determined to go left. Something scurried over my foot and I let out a scream, my glamour falling away like water as I lost hold of it. Had the sensation been a normal forest animal? Or something creepier?

I heard chattering, and then a scratchy voice. "Well, well. What do we have here?"

A goblin. He stood before me, his wrinkled face gazing up. He was so close I could have reached out and touched him.

I opened my mouth to scream again, but nothing came out.

"Cat got your tongue?" He circled me. "I know you. You're supposed to be some great, special faery, aren't you?"

I didn't answer.

"Don't look like nothing special to me."

I swallowed and found my voice. "Leave me alone."

"I don't want to. I have no reason to keep you alive."

He was less than three feet tall. How dangerous could he be? If I could just kick him hard enough, he'd go flying, and I could run. I started backing up very slowly and then suddenly tripped on something—either a branch or my own feet. Pain shot up my leg as I twisted and hit the ground on my butt.

"Damn it," I swore, clutching my ankle.

The goblin was closer now, an evil smile spreading across his face. "Thought you could get out of here, did you? The tree roots here like to move and grow unexpectedly."

I glanced down at my feet and saw the root I had tripped on burrow back into the ground. I scooted backwards, my hand hitting something else. I turned to find a different root emerging from the ground.

"I wouldn't go too far," he cackled. "There's a drop-off just a few feet behind you. You don't want to fall."

I turned my head. Sure enough, after a few more feet of dark forest floor, there was a black darkness where the grass ended. The goblin came closer and fear paralyzed me. It wasn't Adam's face that flashed before me; it was Kallan's. He was who I thought about first.

"Please," I begged. "Please don't hurt me." I tried to get to my feet, but my ankle exploded in pain.

The goblin was closer now. I noticed how creepily long his fingers were as he reached out to touch me.

"Rylie!"

"Kallan!" I yelled back.

Kallan burst through the trees and stuck his dagger into the goblin. The goblin's mouth opened in a silent scream, and he dropped to the ground.

Kallan yanked the dagger out and put it back on

his belt, then rushed to my side. "Are you okay?"

"Yeah...you saved me. Again."

Kallan didn't answer. He extended his hand.

I took it and then yelled out as I placed pressure on my foot. I had forgotten about hurting my ankle.

Wrinkles erupted on his forehead. "What's wrong?"

"My ankle."

He helped me over to a log and sat me down. "Let me see."

"It's too dark."

Kallan dug into his backpack and pulled a long yellow stick from it. He cracked the stick between his hands, and light burst from it like a glow stick—only much brighter. He took my shoe and sock off and poked around on my foot. "I think it's just sprained." He reached back in his backpack and pulled out a disposable ice pack. "Put this on it."

I laughed. "You just happened to have an ice pack in your bag?"

"You're not used to walking through the woods so much. I was worried something would happen." He motioned to my foot and gave me a wry grin. "Unfortunately, I was right."

I settled the ice pack against my ankle and sighed as the cold seeped through my skin. "That feels good. Why were you gone so long?"

"Why weren't you invisible?"

"I got scared and my glamour dropped. This isn't second nature to me like it is you."

"You're right. I shouldn't have left you. If something would have happened to you...." His voice trailed off and pain flickered across his face.

"Did you get what you were after?" I wanted to get out of this part of the woods as quick as possible.

"We got a lead."

I waited, thinking he'd say more, but he didn't. "What is it?"

"You wouldn't understand."

"So?"

He shrugged. "Okay. The faery was seen near the field of rocks."

He was right. I had no clue what that meant. "Where is that?"

"Few hours away. But that ankle is going to present a problem." He pursed his lips. "We could rest here for the night."

I looked around at the eerie forest. "Do we have to?"

Kallan reached back in his bag and pulled out a small green fruit. "If you eat this, your ankle will feel better. Won't be completely healed, but you should be able to walk on it."

"Is this something like what Lena gave me?" Lena was a light faery with healing powers that Varwik held captive by threatening her family. Kallan looked confused, so I added, "When I had a stomachache at your...house?" I wasn't really comfortable calling a castle a "house," but that was where he lived.

"Yes, that drink was made from this fruit."

I took the fruit and bit into it. My stomach churned. "Yuck! That doesn't taste like the drink."

"The drink is made with other things that make it taste better. You gotta finish it though."

I sighed and ate the rest of the fruit, trying not to gag. It was the first faery fruit that I didn't like. After a minute, I felt a warm tingling in my ankle and the throbbing subsided. "Wow. That stuff is pretty awesome."

Kallan helped me stand up. "How does it feel?"

When I put pressure on my foot, the pain was

gone. A smile broke out on my face. "Let's get out of here!"

CHAPTER EIGHTEEN

It didn't take long for us to emerge out of Targore. I breathed a sigh of relief when we stepped into the clearing.

"That place is…" I couldn't put my finger on it.

"Draining," Kallan finished my thought.

"Yes."

"Targore does that. It drains the energy and the happiness from you."

"Yuck."

"We don't go in there much. Nobody likes to."

"I don't want to go back. Do we have to go that way again?"

"It depends on where we end up."

I rolled my eyes at his cryptic answer. If I never saw that part of the forest again, it would be too soon.

"Where are we going to sleep?" I yawned. My whole

body felt exhausted, as if I could curl up in a ball and sleep where we stood.

"There's a town up ahead. We can stay in one of the cottages. I think you'd prefer that over the woods?" He gave me a rascally grin. "You've been softened living in the human realm."

The thought of a soft bed, warm shower, and hot food was enough not to be bothered by his dig. I scoffed. "Look who's talking. You grew up in a castle."

He waggled his eyebrows at me. "Yes, but I'm more at home in the woods. I'd much rather sleep here."

We didn't walk for much longer before we began to see signs of the town. Creatures scurried about. Some looked almost human. Some...not so much.

We left the trees for a cobblestone road whose steep slant caused me to trip, but Kallan grabbed me before I could fall.

I smiled in appreciation. "Thanks."

He pointed at a small stone cottage ahead. The roof was made of grass, and a wooden sign that read "Morian's Hideaway" hung from the doorway. "That's where we'll stay."

"It's cute." I glanced around and noticed most of the buildings were made from stone or wood with grass for roofs. It was quaint.

"I've stayed there before. Morian will be pleased to meet you."

"Me?"

Kallan chuckled. "Everyone knows about you. You're the 'talk of the town' as humans like to say."

Great.

The door swung open before we reached the entrance. A woman with long blonde hair, full lips, and a perfect nose stood in front of us. She would have been beautiful if it weren't for the fact she only had one eye in the middle of her face. As if that wasn't enough, the eye was milky white. "Kallan, dear. How wonderful it is to see you. I see you brought a friend." She smiled over at me.

I looked down at my feet to keep myself from gawking.

"Now, now, dear. Don't be embarrassed. Am I the first cyclops you've come across?" She didn't wait for me to answer the question before asking another. "I can't believe you were raised with humans. Is that really true?" She opened the door wider for us to enter.

"Umm, yeah, it's true. I haven't spent much time in your world."

"Shameful. It really is." She wiped her hands on her apron and pulled Kallan in for a hug. "Don't you look just as handsome as ever."

"You look quite stunning yourself. Is it okay if we crash here for the evening?"

"Of course, but I only have one room available. Will that be a problem?"

Kallan shifted on his feet, obviously uncomfortable.

"That's fine." I would much rather share a room with Kallan than have to worry about goblins and monsters.

Kallan looked at me in surprise, and I just shrugged.

I changed the subject. "I don't mean to sound rude, but do you have anything to eat around here? I'm starving."

Morian grinned. "A girl after my own heart. I love to cook. I have a roast that should be just about ready." She turned and hurried down the hall. When she realized we weren't following, she waved us back.

The cottage was small and the hallway was narrow. I ran my hand down the smooth stones as we made our way to the kitchen.

"Go sit down. The food will be right out." She ushered us towards a darkened room. When we walked in, the candles flickered to life. I looked around, wondering how that had happened. I was starting to realize nothing was unusual in the faery world.

A small wooden table sat in the middle of the floor. Instead of legs, a huge tree trunk formed the base. While it would have looked ridiculous in my own dining room, in this room it was perfect. Kallan pulled out a chair for me, and I dropped into it, relieved to be off my feet. We sat in silence and waited for Morian to return.

The food was delicious. I cleaned my plate and had seconds, which seemed to please Morian. Halfway through the meal, Kallan remembered my injury from my run-in with the goblin, and asked Morian if she could help. She laid her hands on my ankle, and warmth suffused my limb. Moments later, there was no more niggling pain.

After the table was clear, Morian passed a key to Kallan. "You're in room three. Call me if you need anything. I'll be sure to cook up a big breakfast before you take off."

Kallan led me to a short wooden door marked by a brass number 3.

The doorway wasn't very tall, so we both had to duck to enter. A large four-poster bed was off to the right. The room was sparse, but cozy looking. A bright multicolored throw rug covered the floor and soft candlelight cast shadows on the ground.

"Where's the bathroom?" I looked around, not seeing one.

"It's down the hall. Everyone shares."

"Oh. Well, I'm going to clean up." I didn't like the idea of sharing a bathroom with other creatures from the area, but what choice did I have? I was just grateful to have a place to sleep.

I quickly cleaned up and came back to the room. Kallan was lying on the bed with his feet crossed and his hands behind his head. Suddenly, my stomach felt like a field of butterflies was trying to escape.

I swallowed hard and looked around the room. There was no other place to sleep except the floor.

"Have you ever slept with a guy before?" Kallan smirked and patted the bed beside him.

I felt the heat rise to my face. Did he really think I was going to have sex with him? He'd lost his mind.

I tried to play it cool. "It's okay, Kallan. I know you're nervous. You don't have to revert back to the arrogant jerk I met last year."

A look of surprise crossed his beautiful face. "I was just teasing. You have to admit this is awkward."

"Well, it shouldn't be. We've 'slept together.' In the forest, when you helped me escape." I crossed my arms.

"I know, but this just seems more intimate."

"We'll pretend we're outside under the stars." I made my way towards the bed. I hoped I sounded more confident than I felt. "I'm exhausted, Kallan. I need sleep."

"So you're not going to answer my question?" Kallan asked quietly. "Have you ever been with a guy?"

"I really don't think that's any of your business." I wasn't about to admit to him that I was still a virgin. "Have you ever been serious with anyone?"

"I've had girlfriends."

"Serious ones?"

"Not one I've ever opened up to."

Our eyes locked for what seemed like an eternity. Then he rose to his feet and said, "My turn to clean up."

I watched as he walked out the room. He drove me crazy, because I had no idea what he was thinking.

I tossed back the patchwork quilt and got under the covers. The bed was so soft I felt like I was floating on a marshmallow. As soon as my head hit the pillow, I was out like a light.

Next thing I knew, I was waking up with Kallan's arm wrapped around my waist and his chest pressed against my back.

My heart beat wildly even though it felt like I couldn't breathe. I didn't dare move. I could feel the warmth of his body and the strength in his muscles. It took all of my self-control not to turn around and wrap my arms around him. I ached for the feel of his lips on mine.

Adam was the only thing stopping me. I couldn't do that to him.

After what seemed like a lifetime, Kallan started to stir. He pulled his arms back and stretched.

I turned over to look at his face. Even half-asleep, he took my breath away. He opened his sleepy eyes and smiled over at me. And then, as if he realized where he was, his eyes widened.

"Morning," I said cheerfully.

"I thought you weren't a morning person." He rubbed his face.

"I'm not. I've been up for a while. And after sleeping on this soft bed, I can't think of a reason to be grouchy."

Kallan propped his head in his hand and stared at me. "You're something else, you know?"

I didn't know what to say. I tossed the blankets off

and flung my legs off the side of the bed. "We should probably get moving."

Kallan nodded. "Yeah, we'll eat and go."

Breakfast was buffet style and consisted of breads, fruits, and waffles with a rich syrup unlike any I'd ever had. We sat at a table for two and around us were other...creatures, some faeries I could recognize, but others I didn't. It was very odd eating with things that looked like they walked out of some fantasy movie. It didn't help that it felt like everyone was staring at us. I heard the word "Aurorian" whispered a handful of times.

We stepped out of the cottage into the full morning sun. It was warm on my face and I closed my eyes to enjoy it for a moment. Opening them, I smiled at Kallan. "Let's go."

Today had to be better than yesterday.

We walked through the small town on the cobblestone pathway. Carts were being set out for the market, and children ran and played around them. At the edge of the town, we took a well-worn path into the forest. It looked completely different from the side we'd already passed through. I was thrilled to see it wasn't scary at all. I stayed quiet for a while, lost in my thoughts.

As we came upon a small wooden bridge over a wide stream, Kallan turned towards me. "We need to cross this, but you mustn't look down."

"Why not?" I sighed. "What is it this time?"

"You'll be lost. Just hold on to me and get to the other side quickly without looking down." He grabbed my hand and started to cross the bridge.

Don't look down, don't look down, don't look down. As with any normal person telling me not to do something, chanting made me want to do it more. My eyes tried to peek downwards.

"Rylie!" Kallan snapped. "Don't look down!"

I snapped my head back up and focused on what was in front of me.

Once we stepped onto land on the other side, Kallan said, "Do you ever listen?"

"It's been known to happen," I joked, but then turned more serious. "Sorry."

"Just try to comprehend what I'm saying. You know nothing about this realm. I...I don't want to lose you."

I opened my mouth to respond, but shut it instead. I walked past him. "This way?" I asked innocently. I was annoyed, because I knew he was right. I didn't know anything about this realm, or any other realms for that matter.

"Yes." He caught up to me and took the lead again.

"Is there somewhere that might have cell phone service?"

"I don't know. Why?"

"I should call home soon. I'm sure my parents are worried."

"I'll try to find you a place." He continued walking. "It won't be much longer."

Good. I was tired of seeing nothing but trees and dirt, and my feet hurt. I groaned when we started to go uphill.

Kallan laughed, though it sounded like he was trying not to.

The hike upwards didn't take as long as I thought it would. As I set foot at the highest spot, I followed Kallan's gaze to a plateau that was full of very large rocks.

"Are these normal rocks?" I asked.

Kallan looked at me, confused. "What?"

"Or are they like magical rocks? Are they going to move? Or eat me? Anything?"

His eyes laughed. "These are normal rocks. But we have to go across them. And even though they are normal, you could still slip and fall on them."

"Good thing you're here to catch me."

He looked speechless as he helped me onto the first stone. Slowly and carefully, we crossed the rocks. Kallan pointed to what looked like an opening to a cave. He ducked inside and I followed. The narrow entrance widened to a large chamber that resembled a studio apartment. A bed was on the left, a table with a lantern on it was straight ahead, and on the right was a table and chair with someone sitting in it.

"Alven." Kallan called him by name.

The faery stood up, his dark wings flapping behind him. One of them looked damaged. I wondered if he was born that way or if something had happened to him. He had dark hair and eyes. His face was long and thin.

"Interesting," he said, stroking his chin, his gaze taking us in languidly. "The dark prince and the Aurorian came to find me together. To what do I owe this pleasure?"

"If you know who we are, then you know why we're here," Kallan said.

He scoffed. "What faery doesn't know who the two of you are? Even a wanderer like myself has heard all the gossip flying around about you."

"Where is Oren?"

"It is true. I have seen him."

"Tell us! Where is he?" Kallan raised his voice.

"What will you give me for the information?"

"Nothing."

Alven opened his hands as if to say oh well. "Then

you will get no information."

"Do you forget what I can do?" Kallan let go of my hand and stood in front of me, his hand on his dagger. "I can erase your memory...completely. Gone. You won't know a thing when I'm done with you. You'll be left a blubbering fool."

Fear flashed across Alven's face. "Very well. He was east of here, about a day's walk. Exit into the city. I saw him outside of the midwest exit, near Calgren."

Kallan tossed him a gold coin. "For your trouble. Now listen: You never saw us. You never talked to us."

Kallan grabbed my hand and yanked me away. Once we were safely ensconced in the trees, he sighed and closed his eyes.

"Are you okay?" I asked, staring at him intently.

"Yes. You?"

"I'm okay, I guess. It's a lot to take in."

"I'm sure it is for someone who grew up in the human realm, but you're doing great."

He smiled, and my heart fluttered. For some reason, his approval made me happy. I was so worried I was going to screw things up. Everything in the faery land was so foreign to me.

"We need to keep moving," Kallan said, and took off at a brisk pace.

I rushed to keep up. "Do you know how to get where he said?"

"Yes, I've been there before."

"It's not through any scary woods, is it?"

"No. But there are obstacles."

Great. Wasn't there always. "Do I wanna know what they are?"

His large warm hand grasped mine as he helped me down a sloping hill littered with large stones. "Depends. Would you rather be prepared or do you like surprises?"

"Good surprises are different than bad ones." Adam loved to surprise me. Just the thought of him caused a sense of guilt to wash over me.

"Very true." We finally exited the field of rocks. "Mostly it's a long walk."

A long walk I could deal with.

CHAPTER NINETEEN

"This area is called the Four Seasons," Kallan told me as we emerged from the woods into a field that reminded me of spring. Things were budding and coming alive. I could smell the flowers and feel the warm sunshine on my face. It was a beautiful day, and I wanted to sit in the field forever.

About half a mile later, sweat trickled down my back. "It's so hot!" I complained.

"Summer," Kallan stated.

It seemed to get hotter and hotter with every step I took. I fanned myself with my hand, which did absolutely nothing. I grabbed the water bottle out of my bag and took a few gulps, then pulled my hair into a bun to get it off my neck.

"C'mon." Kallan offered me his hand. "Sooner we move, sooner we get through here."

Somehow I managed to put one foot in front of the other and continued to walk. It must have been a mile until I felt cooler and the scents changed. The beautiful red, orange, and yellow leaves on the trees around us drifted to the ground. Almost as if they were dancing.

Up ahead, I saw something white floating down from the sky. "Is that...?"

"Snow."

A few minutes later, we reached the snow-covered field. What started as a few snowflakes turned into a blizzard. My teeth were chattering within minutes. My fingers and toes were numb. And my body ached to go back to summer, no matter how hot it was.

Kallan pulled me close to him. Together, we trudged through the high snow until it gradually became lower and lower, and then it was just gone and the temperature turned normal again.

"Well, that was...interesting."

Kallan faced me. "Life is different here. Do you think you'll ever get used to it?"

I reached up and brushed the snow off his hair, leaving it wet and messy. Our faces were just inches apart, and I so wanted to kiss him. I swallowed hard and answered, "I might be able to. It'll probably take a while though."

As we walked, I asked, "So how do you like the human world?"

He cleared his throat. "I don't especially like it."

"I get the sense you don't hate it, though."

"No. I don't hate it. The area where you live is nice. I guess I feel like you do: it's different and hard to get used to, but not impossible."

I understood that. "I hope you'll give it a chance. There is some good there."

He nodded. "This way."

We left the forest and emerged into a dark alley. I

looked around, confused. Where were we? How did we get from nature to an alleyway with tall buildings on both sides? "How did...? Where are we?"

Kallan chuckled. "A faery gateway."

"What is that?"

"There are different ways to get in and out of the faery realm. Shortcuts, if you will," he explained. "You can call home now."

I slid my hand in my pocket and pulled out my cell phone. As soon as I turned it on, it started chiming letting me know I had voicemails and texts. There were at least a dozen from my parents, a couple from Sierra, and one from Adam. I listened to them all, saving Adam's for last.

"I've been trying to call you, but your voicemail keeps picking up. I don't know what's going on. I thought we were going to hang out before I leave for California, but when I went to your house your parents said you went with a family member. They were acting kinda strange. Um...I hope you're okay. Call me...please. Love you."

I couldn't look at Kallan. The concerned sound of Adam's voice hit me hard. Why did this have to be so confusing? I saved the message and then called home.

"Hello?" Mom answered frantically.

"Hey, Mom."

"Rylie! Are you okay? Where are you? What is going on?" Her tone was borderline hysterical.

I cringed. "I'm fine. I'm not really sure where I am. I just wanted to let you know I'm okay. I know I left without talking to you. I'm sorry. I just...I need to do this. And I need for you to understand. I'll be back soon, I promise."

"Rylie...come home now. Please." Her voice cracked.

"I can't. Not yet. This week is spring break so I won't miss any school. I'll be home before then. I promise."

I heard her sigh. "Are you safe?"

I glanced at Kallan. There was no doubt in my mind that he'd keep me safe. "Yes. I've gotta go. I'll call again soon. I love you." I hung up before she could say anything else. I powered the phone down so the battery wouldn't die and shoved it back into my pocket.

"Everything okay?"

"Yeah. They're upset."

"They're worried." He ran the back of his hand down my cheekbone, causing me to take a long shuddering breath.

"So where are we?"

"Should be near Oklahoma City."

"What? Oklahoma? What are we doing in Oklahoma?"

"This is where Oren was spotted."

So he was close. I took a deep breath. My biological father lived somewhere nearby, and I would meet him soon. That scared the hell out of me.

It was nightfall in the human realm. The lights from the city were so bright I couldn't see the stars above. "What do we do now?"

Kallan took a deep breath. "Are you tired?"

I nodded. "Exhausted. We did a lot of walking today."

"There are plenty of hotels around."

Once again, the thought of a soft bed and real food made my whole body relax. "I like the sound of that."

He led me down a narrow side road and around the corner onto a busy main street. He stepped into the road and hailed a cab. Twenty minutes later, we were checked into a hotel. Once again, they only had one bed available, and I wondered if Kallan was somehow arranging that.

The room was cool and dim. I sat down on the bed and kicked my shoes off my aching feet. Using my thumbs, I started rubbing them, hoping to ease the pain.

"Here. Let me." Kallan took my feet in his hands and began to massage them. His hands were like magic.

I closed my eyes and leaned back against the headboard. "It feels wonderful."

I drifted off under his touch. After a few minutes, I felt something being placed on top of me. Opening my eyes, I saw he had pulled a blanket up to my shoulders. I smiled and went back to sleep.

When I opened them again, I found Kallan staring at me. He was lying next to me, one corner of his mouth turned up. He reached out and pushed back some hair that was in my face.

"Morning," he whispered.

Light filtered through the small openings in the curtains. "Guess I really was tired."

"Why don't you take a shower, and I'll order room service."

I rubbed the sleep from the corners of my eyes. "Coffee. Get lots of coffee."

"Got it."

I flipped the covers off and stumbled into the bathroom. I closed the door behind me and let my hand linger on the doorknob as I thought about Kallan. What was I doing here with him? He was wiggling his way into every aspect of my life, and I was enjoying it. I envisioned myself opening the door back up, walking back to where he was, and kissing him.

No, no, no. Focus. Today is the day I meet my father.

I thought about that—finding out why he traded me, and what he was planning to do now. Maybe this wasn't a good idea. What was I thinking, taking off on my own like this? I glanced over at Kallan and realized I was far from being alone, but that didn't stop me from being any less scared.

We hopped on a bus and rode for about half an hour, getting off at the last stop. It was a rural area with large open farmland. A single wooden mailbox was on the side of the street with the name NERO in large gold letters.

"Why is his name backwards?" I asked Kallan.

"We don't have last names like you do. He probably turned it around just to blend in with humans."

"Oh." I hadn't realized that before.

As we walked further up the dirt road, a small house appeared. There was no car in the driveway, and I wondered if anyone would even be home.

I heard a strange thudding in the distance, and glanced over at Kallan. "What's that?"

He put a finger to his lips. Quietly, we went around the back of the house. A faery, axe in hand, stood over a log chopping wood. He seemed to sense our presence immediately. His body stiffened. Slowly, he turned and faced us.

His light brown hair was cut short, almost buzzed. He rested the axe against his broad shoulder. He wasn't at all what I was expecting. In my mind, my father was a weak flower-smeller. A coward who ran away and left his wife. The man standing before us looked like a warrior. His body was strong and his blue eyes were cold. Maybe we were at the wrong house.

Nobody spoke. It was one of the most awkward

moments I had ever experienced.

The faery's eyes narrowed. "Get out of here," he growled.

I almost turned and left. But then Kallan's voice rang out. "Oren? You are Oren, right? I'm..."

He stared at my birthmark. "I know who you are. How did you find me? Who sent you?" He took a step closer.

My eyes rested on the axe he still held in his hands. I swallowed hard, wondering if he'd actually use it. Surely my own father wouldn't kill me. He had traded me, but could he be a murderer as well?

Kallan took a step in front of me. Having him there gave me strength. "We just want to talk," he said evenly.

"Nobody ever just wants to talk."

I took a chance and walked closer to him. Kallan followed. It wasn't until I was standing a couple feet from him that I could see the age in his face. Wrinkles spread near his eyes and forehead. He had not aged as well as Azura, that much was obvious. But the weathered look only added to his cold demeanor. My eyes were drawn to his vibrant orange and white wings. This stranger was my father. I felt anger course through my body. He had walked away and moved on with his life.

He knew who I was and didn't seem all that shocked that his thought-to-be-dead daughter was standing before me. If anything, he seemed annoyed.

"Why?" I asked, so low I could barely hear my own voice.

As if my words pulled him out of a trance, he shook his head and looked in my eyes. "What?"

"Why? That's all I want to know. I'll leave you alone. Won't bother you again. I just want to know why you traded me. Your own flesh and blood."

"I can't tell you that." He ran his large hand over his face.

"Can't or won't?" I glared at him.

He stood in place, steady as a rock. His face was cold and hard, and his body rigid.

I pressed my lips together and spun on my heels. I had to stop myself from breaking into a run, to get far away from this place. Before I could, fury rose within me.

Turning back to face him, I yelled, "How could you do what you did? Do you have any idea what it has done to my life? I am your daughter! Don't you care? Varwik will kill me if I don't marry Kallan. All because of your greed."

Guilt flashed across his face, but was quickly replaced by coldness. "I don't owe either of you an explanation."

"I hate you! I hate you for everything you have done to Azura, to me, to my parents. You make me sick. You are a poor excuse for a man."

"I said get out of here!" he barked through gritted teeth.

That time, I didn't hesitate. I grabbed Kallan's hand and ran like hell. At the end of the long road, Kallan pulled me to a stop. "We don't have to run."

"I know. I just...I had to get out of there as fast as possible. I can't believe that man is my father."

He nodded in understanding. "I didn't expect him to be such a jackass. He could have at least shown some remorse. I was so tempted to use my power on him, but I wouldn't do that without your permission."

"He's not worth it." I wiped a tear from my face.

"Do you want to go home now?"

I shook my head, blinded by the hot tears pouring out of my eyes. "No. I can't face my parents right now." I wiped my face with my hands and looked up at Kallan. "Could we go back to the hotel?"

"Of course."

I tried to keep it together the rest of the way there. I didn't want strangers staring at me. As soon as the door closed behind us, the tears started flowing again. Kallan put his strong arms around me, and I sobbed into his chest.

After a few minutes, he coaxed me over to the bed and helped me to sit. I looked into his eyes. "Why does it hurt so much?"

"Oh, Rylie. I'm so sorry..." He leaned closer and kissed under my eyes. I could feel his warm breath on my lips as he pressed his forehead to mine, and I desperately wanted him to kiss me.

Instead, he pulled away, his jaw clenched. "Not like this, Rylie. I want to kiss you, but I want you to kiss me, too."

He leaned against the headboard and patted the bed next to him. I scooted to sit beside him, and laid my head against his chest. With one hand, he stroked my hair and with the other he fiddled with the TV remote.

"Kallan, I feel lost and hopeless."

"Shhh, it's okay."

"Thank you for helping me. I know it can't be easy. If we break the promise..."

"I told you, Rylie. I want you to be with me because it's your choice, not my father's."

I laid my head against his shoulder and closed my eyes. I was mentally and physically exhausted. It was just too much to take in. My whole world had been turned around ever since Azura knocked on my door. Unable to keep my eyes open, I drifted off to sleep.

I woke up lying next to Kallan, and it felt so natural—so safe. Part of me wanted to stay snuggled up for as long as I possibly could. I could forget about light and dark faeries, forget about promises and my dad and all the other worries floating about in my mind.

My stomach had other plans, however. It let out a powerful growl.

Kallan nudged me with a chuckle. "You awake?"

"Yes," I admitted.

"Sounds like you're hungry."

I turned over to grin at him. "I guess I am."

"Well, let's go eat."

"You have somewhere in mind?"

A slow smile spread across his handsome face. "I do love French toast. That's one thing humans got right."

"Room service or eat out?" I asked, sitting up in the bed.

"Whatever you want."

I didn't have to think too hard. "Let's find a local diner. Whenever I go on a trip with my parents, we love to try out mom and pop places."

"Mom and pop?"

"Local places owned by small business owners instead of big chains," I explained. "My parents have always been big on showing support for the American dream."

"Your parents sound like good people."

"They are." And they were probably out of their minds with worry. The reminder was a stark one, and it crash-landed me back into the real world.

Once in the lobby, we asked the receptionist to point us in the right direction. There was a place called Coffee Dive down the street. We made our way, lost in our own thoughts.

The bell jingled as we walked through the single, smeared-glass door. The Coffee Dive was a small, dimly lit diner with warm, orange walls and white tables on a black-and-white checkered floor. A curvy woman with red hair piled high above a heart-shaped face and a white apron tied around her hourglass waist smiled from behind the counter. "Welcome. You're obviously not from around here."

I looked at Kallan. "What gave it away?"

"Youngsters don't wander in here unless they're with family." The woman chuckled. "We're not exactly the hot spot in town."

"Receptionist at the hotel said you had the best coffee in town," Kallan commented.

"Damn right!" she said proudly. "Find a seat and make yourself at home."

We picked a table in the corner. There were only a few people eating—a couple near the door with a toddler, a table full of gossiping women near the counter, and an old man with a newspaper, but mostly, it was quiet. A country song played on the antique jukebox.

"I can see why your parents like to visit places like this." Kallan's eyes met mine across the table. "After my mother died, we no longer took part in any family traditions."

"I'm sorry."

"Don't be. It was a long time ago." He unrolled his silverware and arranged it on top of his napkin as he went on. "Maybe this can be a tradition for us. Checking out new places off the beaten path."

His words took me by surprise. The thought of making new traditions with Kallan was the furthest thing from my mind, but in reality, next year I could be his wife. With that came those kinds of things—traditions, celebrations, kids...

I was only a kid myself. I couldn't think about that right now.

"Maybe," I mumbled, relieved that the waitress had returned with coffee.

She set the mugs in front of us and poured from a steaming carafe. "Y'all know what you're having?"

She took our orders for French toast and then bustled off. The brief interlude gave me a chance to change the subject. "We didn't learn anything. By going to Oren's, I mean."

"We'll figure it out."

"Feels like a wasted trip. All that way for nothing."

Kallan hmmed noncommittally.

"How do we get home?" I asked.

"You don't want to try to talk to Oren again?"

"I can't. Not right now." Absently, I rearranged the sweeteners in the container by color. I even removed two sugar packets stained with old coffee, and tossed them aside to be thrown away.

"Okay," Kallan responded, surprising me.

"You aren't going to argue with me?"

He cocked an eyebrow. "Why would I argue? It's your father and your life. I just came to..."

"To what?"

Kallan cleared his throat, and when he answered, I could have sworn there was a blush in his cheeks. "To be with you. To protect you."

I didn't really know what to say, so for the fifth time, I changed the subject. "So...how do we go home?"

"We can go back the way we came."

"Do we really have to go back the same way?" I shuddered, thinking of the creatures lurking along that path through the faery world.

Kallan's lips curved up. "It's the easiest."

I scowled and lowered my voice. "I don't like it."

"We could return the human way, I suppose."

"Really?"

"If it would make you feel better."

"That would be so awesome. But...how?"

"How what?"

"We're in Oklahoma! How are we going to get back to Virginia?"

"We fly."

I looked up at his wings, my skin growing cold. I'd never really tried to fly. There was no way!

His teal eyes twinkled in the sunlight. "Not that way. In a plane. I have an account set up for when I'm in the human realm. Money isn't an issue."

"Oh. Good to know." I had wondered how we were paying for the hotel room and food. I thought maybe he had been using his mind control power, and now I knew he wasn't. For some reason, that made me feel better about him. Knowing that he could have used his powers but didn't, that meant something.

"We'll go in the morning."

"I should call home." I pulled out my phone and turned it on. Again, messages poured in. I pushed the button and listened to the phone ring.

"Hello?"

"Mom, it's me. I'll be home tomorrow."

"Rylie! Thank God. Where are you?"

"I'm okay. Don't worry. I'll be home sometime to-morrow. We'll talk then."

I heard her sigh. "Okay. We love you."

"I love you, too." After I hung up, I caught Kallan's gaze and said, "I feel so awful."

"Why?" Kallan asked.

"I've put them through so much. None of this has been fair to them. Not what Azura did and not what I'm doing now."

"You're only doing what you feel you have to."

I turned away from his gaze and stared out into the street. "Doesn't make it right."

That night, I slept fitfully, tossing and turning every which way. My dreams were haunting: full of faeries and shadows as I ran through the dark forest of the faery world.

I jerked awake when I felt the bed move, my heart still pounding. I looked over my shoulder to see Kallan climbing in next to me.

"What are you doing?" I asked him, my voice groggy with sleep.

"Shhh. Just close your eyes and relax."

I stared into his eyes for a minute, and then slowly rested my head back on my pillow and closed my eyes. His arms wrapped around me as he snuggled his warm body next to mine. He ran his hand up and down my wings so that tingles ran through my body. But the motion soothed my fears, and soon, I was asleep.

CHAPTER TWENTY

We stood in front of my house. The light was on in the living room and both cars were in the driveway. I needed to go in, but I wanted to linger outside with Kallan a little longer. "Thanks for coming with me."

"Anytime. I'll always be there when you need me. Are you sure you're going to be okay?"

When Kallan said things like that, it warmed my heart. "Yeah. I just need some time to process everything."

"Let me know if I can help," he offered sincerely.

"I will. Thanks." I turned to go, but spun back around. "It's been nice, ya know?"

"What has?" His lips quirked up slightly.

"Being with you these past few days."

Kallan's cheeks turned pink. "I enjoyed your company too." He reached forward and ran his hand down one of my wings. That wonderful thrill went through my body, and I closed my eyes to hide how much I liked it. "You could come home with me now."

Part of my body screamed "yes!" but rational me stomped that part out. "I can't," I muttered. "Not yet." I still wanted to find a way out of the promise.

Kallan nodded, disappointment in his eyes. "I know."

"I'm sorry." I hurried up the steps and into the house before he could say any more. I was afraid he'd say something that would lure me to his world sooner than I was supposed to.

The door slammed shut behind me.

"Rylie?" Mom's voice drifted from the kitchen.

"Yeah," I answered meekly.

There was a beat of silence before my parents both rushed into the hallway and threw their arms around me. The hug was tight and filled with grateful greetings and a teary "Thank you, God" from my mother.

After a minute, Dad stepped away and looked over me. "Are you hurt?"

I shook my head.

"Hungry?"

Again, I shook no.

He sighed. "I'm not sure if I should be happy or mad."

"I'm sorry." When my eyes filled with tears, I got angry at myself and took a deep breath to fight them off.

"Why?" my father asked.

"To get some questions answered."

My father's face softened. "I could have helped you if you had to get answers. We could have found them together."

"I'm not sure you could have," I told him.

Mom stood beside him, her arms wrapped around her chest as she sniffled. "What kind of answers?"

"We had to talk to some..." I paused, not knowing what I wanted to tell them, "creatures in the faery land to find out where he was."

"Creatures?"

"Yeah."

Mom and Dad exchanged glances, and she said softly, "I don't like the sound of that."

Dad put a hand on Mom's shoulder. "Did you find what you were looking for?"

I remembered Oren's ambivalence. His cold eyes. "I found..."

I must have trailed off and been silent for too long, because Dad asked sharply, "What, Rylie?"

"My biological father. My faery father."

I watched as my father's face transformed from concerned father to wounded puppy. Mom, who must have known how he felt after learning about Azura, slipped an arm around his waist in support.

"And?" she asked.

"He didn't want to talk."

"That's it?" Dad asked.

"He made it very clear he didn't want to be bothered."

"Oh, honey." Mom came forward and ran her hands down my hair, then cupped my face. "That must have been hard to hear."

"I just wanted answers, not a relationship. I guess I won't be getting either." I shrugged. "Is it okay if I go call Adam and Sierra?"

Mom opened her mouth to speak, but Dad put a hand on her arm to silence her. "Yes, but we have something to say first."

"Okay."

"You can't just take off like that, so you're grounded for two weeks."

I was shocked. My parents had never grounded me like that before. Maybe for a day or two, but never weeks. Then again, I hadn't taken off before. But I wasn't stupid; I knew I deserved it. I nodded. "Okay."

"Seriously," Dad said. "No more running off. I think you know we're as understanding as we can be about all of this. Just come talk to us. We'll try to work something out."

"You do need to go see Azura though," Mom said. Dad shot her a look. "She's been very worried about you, and I'm sure you need to tell her what happened."

"Probably should," I agreed.

Dad spoke up again. "Other than that, you're grounded."

"I get it."

Mom hugged me one more time. "We're glad you're home, sweetie."

My shoulders slumped as I trudged up the stairs. In my room, I took a deep breath. The smell of home filled my lungs and made me smile. Grounded or not, I was happy to be back. I plugged in my cell phone and called Adam first. Thankfully, my parents didn't take my phone away, too.

"Rylie?" he answered, his voice betraying not only worry but irritation.

"Hi."

"Where have you been?"

"Family issues."

"You seem to be saying that a lot lately," he said hotly. In a more even tone, he went on. "Are your parents okay?"

"Yeah. It's a long story."

"Why didn't you call me?"

"I...couldn't. What have you been doing?"

There was a long moment where I thought he was

going to push me for answers. If he got too direct with the questions, I wouldn't be able to evade him since I couldn't lie. I knew it wasn't fair to him that I disappeared for two days and didn't call or text. If he thought badly of me for it, I wouldn't blame him. I hadn't been the best girlfriend lately.

Finally, Adam sighed. "Touring the college, sightseeing, stuff like that."

Oh, right! He was checking out Southern Cal to see if he really wanted to go to school there. "I'm sorry," I told him sadly, and I was. "It's a good thing you're not here."

"Why?" His voice was incredulous.

"I'm grounded," I told him.

"You're what?"

"Grounded for two weeks."

"What did you do? It must have been bad. You never get grounded."

"Family issues."

"That's all you're going to say?" he said angrily.

"That's what it is."

I hated myself. Not just for being unable to come clean with Adam about Azura and my heritage, but for the time I'd just spent with Kallan and the way we'd cuddled as if we were already married. Adam didn't deserve this, so I couldn't very well be mad at him for being mad at me.

Adam let out a long breath, as if his anger were deflating. "So I won't be able to see you Sunday?"

"No. I'm so sorry."

"I guess it won't be so bad waiting one more day."

"I miss you," I said honestly.

"I miss you, too."

After we hung up, I called Sierra and told her the same thing, only in a little more detail since she knew my secret.

"I can't believe he was so mean," she said after I told her what Oren had said to me.

"I guess he just hates me. Maybe because I'm the reason he's an outcast? Or the reason he never got the dark magick he wanted so badly."

"Still...that's no way to treat your flesh and blood."

I couldn't argue with her. "So now I have to go tell Azura what happened and then spend the next two weeks grounded."

"That sucks about being grounded."

"Yup."

"Ry," Sierra continued, "I want to come with you."

I groaned. "I don't know if you can."

"Please?" Sierra whined. "My life sucks. I want to visit your faery world. It sounds so magical. Like anything can happen, you know?"

"I'm afraid you might be disappointed."

Sierra's laughter pealed across the phone line. "Let me make that decision. But somehow I doubt it. I've spent the last few months babysitting when I wanted to be on dates or hanging out with you. Getting up in the middle of the night when my sister wouldn't. I need adventure." Her voice grew quiet. "I need an escape, Ry."

I punched my pillow once, but it didn't really vent my frustrations as well as I'd hoped. "I'm going to have to go talk to someone. Figure out a way to get you there."

"I thought you're supposed to be this big shot over there. Like future queen or something."

I laughed. "Not yet. And I didn't grow up there. I don't really know what's possible. Will you give me some time to figure out what I can do?"

"You'll let me know?"

"Of course."

"Okay."

"Look, I gotta go see Azura. Talk to you later?"

"Sure."

After we said our goodbyes, I looked out the window towards the forest. I had a lot to tell Azura, and I wasn't sure how she was going to react to the news about Oren.

Better get this over with sooner rather than later.

CHAPTER TWENTY-ONE

I wasn't sure where I was going. I wasn't positive I could find my way to Azura's house, though I liked the idea of trying anyway—trying to see if I could make it happen.

It didn't matter, because I found Azura in the forest on her cell phone.

"Yes, Angela, she's here now. I will. Thank you. Goodbye." She tapped the screen on her phone and slid it into her pocket, giving me a warm smile. "Your mom called to tell me you were coming. She was worried about you in the woods alone."

"Oh." There went my plan to prove to myself I could find my way to the faery world by myself.

Azura held a hand out, indicating for us to start walking. "Shall we go talk?"

I nodded. "Yes."

The silent walk to her house took no time at all.
Soon, we were seated at her kitchen table, both of us

with glasses of juice and a basket full of freshly baked rolls. I launched into my tale.

When I got to the part where Oren told me to go away, Azura gasped, her face hardening.

"So we left and came home," I finished, my hands kneaded together in my lap and my juice long forgotten. Dredging up that meeting between Oren and me had shaken me. I didn't want it to affect me, but it did.

Azura was quiet for a minute, then she said, "I apologize for the way he treated you."

"It's not your fault."

"I feel that it is." She patted my hand. "How did he look?"

"Different than what I thought. Strong, but old."

"If he's been in the human world, he's aged faster." She glanced out the window. "I was hoping you'd get the answers you wanted."

"'Disappointment is part of life.'" I quoted my dad.

"Mmm."

I'd said my piece about Oren, so now I had to ask a favor for my best friend. "Remember when you said it might be okay to bring Sierra here?"

"Yes," Azura said hesitantly.

"Is it okay? She really wants to come, and I feel I owe her for keeping my secret. She's always there for me—no matter what."

"This means a lot to you?"

I nodded. "It really does."

She took a deep breath. After a couple minutes, she answered, "Okay. You'll have to talk to your cousins."

"Why?"

"They're the ones to help get her here without harm." She shrugged. "Very well, Oleander. Your friend may come."

"Really?"

"Yes. Really."

"Thank you!" I haphazardly threw my arms around her, and then realized what I had just done. I stepped back. "Sorry...I...uh..."

"It's okay. I'm glad I could make you happy." Her lips were curved in a soft smile.

I chided myself for showing so much emotion. Azura was okay. In fact, I was learning to like her. But my mom was still my mom and I didn't want Azura to get any ideas that I'd be moving here.

She glanced out the kitchen window, and then smiled. "Why don't you go outside for a while? Enjoy the twilight and search out your cousins."

That sounded like a good idea. I finished my now-warm juice, stood up, and placed the empty cup in the sink before I headed outside.

There was an energy in the sweet-smelling air, like the electricity before a thunderstorm. As I skipped down the cobblestone pathway behind Azura's house, I took several deep breaths, and for some reason, felt immediately better.

There were no sounds here like there were at home. No traffic passing in the neighborhood, no planes casting shadows on the ground as they angled in to land at the airport. There was a beautiful absence of noise.

I saw Nessa and Violet in the field next door. Violet had an easel and a canvas set up and was painting while Nessa lolled on the grass with a handful of wildflowers. I cut through Azura's garden of herbs, touching the blooming heads of chamomile and lavender, then jumped the white picket fence into their yard

"Hi, Oleander," Nessa greeted me as I walked up.

"Hi." I tried to put on a cheerful face. "What are

you doing?"

"Painting," Violet said in a "duh" voice.

I laughed. "Well, yeah, I see that. I didn't know you could paint."

Violet shrugged. "There's a lot we don't know about each other. We'll catch up over time." She put her brush down on the edge of the easel and turned to look into my eyes, flipping her long blonde hair out of her face. "Heard about your trip."

"Who hasn't?" I asked.

"Nobody."

I laughed to myself, and then hesitated. I hated asking a favor of them when I hardly knew them. "Azura told me you two could help me get a human friend to this realm."

Violet's eyes grew big. "Who?"

"My best friend, Sierra."

"Oh. Thought you might be bringing your boyfriend here."

"No. He doesn't know about me yet. About this."

Nessa crossed her legs Indian-style on the emerald grass. "You gonna tell him?"

I shrugged. "I don't know."

"This Sierra knows about us?"

"Yes."

"She can be trusted?"

"Yes. I trust her with my life."

"I don't know if it's such a great idea. Humans don't belong in our world," Nessa said uncertainly.

I felt panic rise in my chest. They couldn't tell me no. It was too important to Sierra and I wasn't going to let her down.

"I agree with Nessa," Violet said with more conviction.

I glanced back and forth between the two of them,

hoping they were joking, but their faces were set.

"I didn't want to have to do this, but you know with my power I can use yours and get her in here anyway. But I'd really prefer your help," I threatened, but in reality I had no idea how to use their powers.

They looked at each other and then back at me and shrugged. "Okay. We can make something for her to be able to get here. But you'll be responsible for her."

A smile spread across my face. "Thanks, guys."

I left them to their project and wandered around the fields a while longer, taking in the sights and smells. My mind was in overdrive. Human world or fey world? What would I do here in this world? Would I be bored? So much time and not a lot to do. Or maybe there was a lot going on behind the scenes, stuff I didn't see right now.

In an ideal world, I would be able to merge the two.

When I got back to Azura's house, she was standing at the kitchen counter stirring a bowl of what looked like cake batter.

"Were you able to find your cousins?" she asked, offering me a spoon to lick.

"Yes. They're brainstorming." I stuck the spoon in my mouth and groaned. "Heavenly."

"I am a bit worried about your friend coming, but I'm also delighted to be able to entertain a human in my own home." Azura pulled an already buttered cake pan close and picked up the bowl to dump the batter in. "Will you stay for dinner and cake, Oleander?"

I gave her a hug, just a quick squeeze around the shoulders. "I'd love to."

After dinner and a slice of moist chocolate cake, I helped Azura do dishes.

The water sloshed in the sink as Azura pulled out the last clean dish and passed it to me to rinse and dry. "Would you like to stay the night, Oleander?"

I shook my head. "No, I need to get home. I'm in enough trouble as it is."

"I'm so sorry to hear that." She sighed, pulling the drain plug to empty the sink. "I can't help but feel that is entirely my fault."

"No, it's not. I chose to chase after Oren."

Azura dried her hands, eyeing me with affection on her face. She touched my cheek. "Let's get you home."

We walked out of the tree house and into the forest, where birds chirped and piskies fluttered around, trying to entice us. Their sparkling, colorful forms made me think of Kallan.

Azura startled me out of my thoughts. "Thank you for coming and talking with me."

I nodded. "I wanted you to hear it firsthand. Although it seems word travels fast around here"

"That it does. But I still appreciate hearing it from you. I guess I didn't want to believe that Oren could be so cruel to his own daughter."

"He's a real winner," I said wryly, trying to lighten the mood.

"He wasn't always that way." Azura looked down at the ground. "But he gave me you."

Only to be taken away. I kept those thoughts to myself. "I still want out of the promise," I said.

"I know. I'll keep working on it. There has to be a way. Something we are overlooking."

"I hope so. Time is passing so quickly."

"We'll figure it out."

Everyone kept saying that, but no one was coming up with solutions.

"Want to try something?" Azura stopped and turned to me with a sparkle in her eye.

"Um...sure?" I responded curiously.

"Since we're out here, I thought it might be neat to use our powers together."

"Really?"

She raised her hands in response and the wind picked up. A sudden small breeze whipped by my face, tousling my hair. "Do as I do."

I raised my hands like hers. I swirled my arms like she did. A second wind sprang up, sending a few flower petals flying. "Cool," I whispered.

"Now make it grow." She spread her arms, and I copied.

The tall grass and bushes nearby rustled. The two merged together into one big windstorm. Azura was on one side, and I was on the other. It began to take shape like that of a twister, only about ten feet high. The trees on either side began to bend and shake.

"Now drop your arms and let it diminish."

I dropped my arms to my side and the small twister fell apart, gone just as quickly as it had started. "That was awesome."

A smile spread across her face. "It's a powerful talent. It is stronger when you are with me."

"I'd like to do that again sometime," I said breathlessly as we started walking again.

"As long as you remember it's not a toy. A powerful wind can cause a twister to get out of control."

"I understand."

My house was visible up ahead, just through the tree line. Azura squeezed my hand. "Be safe."

I nodded and turned to go, surprised to find that

I was sad to leave Azura behind.

Later that night, I lay in bed unable to sleep.

There was some strange part of me that longed for the faery world. I felt safe there, and I wasn't sure what that meant. It wasn't like I didn't feel a part of the human world, but lately, my heart felt like it was being torn in half. I was changing, and that terrified me.

I couldn't keep doing what I was doing to either Adam or Kallan. It wasn't right. Kallan had the advantage because he knew everything. Adam didn't have a clue what was going on, and frankly, I was lucky he'd put up with my crap the last few weeks.

It was no longer a matter of figuring out what I needed to do. I still had no intention of being forced to marry anyone. I had to find the loophole.

I got out of bed and went to the window. It was dark outside. No sparkling lights or soft glow from the trees. Part of me wished I had grown up with Azura. If I had been born a normal faery instead of an Aurorian faery, none of this would have happened. I wouldn't be torn right now. Maybe I'd be matched up with one of the light faeries I'd recently met.

Of course, then I wouldn't know Sierra, Adam, and my parents. That didn't seem like the perfect world either.

There had to be a way to keep us all together. Except not all of us could be. Either Kallan or Adam had to go.

CHAPTER TWENTY-TWO

I spent the rest of the weekend getting ready for school to start back while I obeyed my grounding by only talking to Adam and Sierra on the phone. By the time Monday morning rolled around, I hurried to school faster than I'd ever done before, excited to see Adam.

He stood on the front steps like he always did. Steady and dependable. I threw my arms around him and gave him a long, passionate kiss.

"Hi," he said with a laugh as we pulled apart.

"Hi. It's so good to be in your arms."

"They're here for you anytime."

Guilt washed over me. "I'm sorry I've been distant. Lots of family things going on."

"Your family is the most normal one I've ever known," Adam said.

It was once, I thought sadly. "All families have secrets."

"I wish you'd tell me what's going on."

"I know. I'm sorry. It's complicated."

The bustling hallway, complete with squeaky sneakers and yelling students, was a welcoming sound. Being back at school made me feel almost normal. Spending the day with Adam, regardless of the fact we were in class, centered me.

I was allowed to go to choir rehearsals, but not Adam's practices. I spent each afternoon doing schoolwork, and as much of the day with Adam that I could. I was able to push Kallan from my mind and forget the way we had bonded while we were away.

It would have continued to work if he hadn't shown up for school on Wednesday.

I avoided him as much as I could, which was the hardest thing ever. Every time I saw him, my wings would remind me how attracted to him I was. It was as if there were some invisible force pulling us together. It got harder and harder to resist as the days passed.

"You're not being fair," Sierra said as she caught me staring at Kallan in the lunchroom. Adam had gone to get us fresh sodas because the two we'd grabbed weren't cold.

I let my head fall into my arms on the tabletop. "I know."

"What are you going to do?" she asked.

"I don't know." It was as simple as that.

"Do you have feelings for Kallan?" Sierra's face told me she already knew the answer.

I nodded.

"But you still love Adam."

"Yeah."

Sierra whistled. "You're in a bad way."

"Tell me about it."

It was finally the end of my grounding and I'd have a whole weekend to catch up on my social life. I sat on the front porch swing with *The Great Gatsby* and a glass of lemonade. It was a warm afternoon after school, and all I had to do was read a chapter, then homework was done for the day.

With an end in sight, I was completely focused on reading. I never heard him approach until his voice broke through my concentration.

"Oleander."

Startled, I dropped my book to my lap and jerked my head up.

Oren.

He looked different than the last time I saw him. His face was softer and his eyes kinder. There was a wariness to his stance. He was guarded.

"What are you doing here?" I asked softly, my heart stopping. Was he going to kidnap me and take me to Varwik?

Oren held up his hands. "I just need to explain. I hope you'll hear me out."

I crossed my arms and waited. Inside, my heart was pounding so hard I thought it would burst through my chest. I couldn't believe he had the nerve to show up at my house, of all places. Thankfully, my real dad wasn't home. He would totally flip out.

"I was a selfish, arrogant man. I had been put down and made fun of all of my life. People teased me for having a stupid talent—making fragrances. I guess it began to wear on me…"

"Excuses," I interrupted, my irritation growing to anger.

"Yes, they are excuses," he agreed. "But it's also the true and honest reason why I did what I did. I'm not trying to say I wasn't wrong."

"Good, then you aren't a complete jerk."

"I deserve that." Oren rubbed his brow and went on. "I tried to change my talent. I visited all the elders, anyone I thought might be able to help me. I dabbled in dark magick, what I could access, to see if I could get a different power. I found nothing to help me. I was depressed and mad at the world. Your mother was the only good in my life, and I treated her like crap because I couldn't accept who I was."

He paused, but I remained silent.

"When Azura told me she was pregnant, I was overjoyed. I decided to stop searching for a better talent and learn how to be a good husband and father. I hoped for a little girl who would sit on my knee while I told stories and taught her everything I know." He smiled at me. "I couldn't wait to teach you our ways, the way my father taught me."

Tears filled my eyes. I tried to blink them away, angry that he was having this effect on me after he did what he did.

"And then you were born. For a few minutes, everything was right with the world. You were so little and so beautiful. I had never been prouder. You fit in the crook of my arm." His face lit up as he spoke. "Then I saw the mark. It triggered a memory of a conversation I had in my quest to find a more powerful talent. Varwik had said he would do anything for the power an Aurorian faery would bring. And there you were, an Aurorian. All I had to do was hand you over..." He choked on his words and made no attempt to wipe away the tears that were running down his face. "I don't know what happened. I just snapped. I could taste the dark magick on my tongue. I argued with myself that we could have more children, and I'd be even better because I'd be more powerful. So I left to make the deal."

I swallowed hard. I wasn't sure if I wanted to hear all this, but it was like a horror movie. Too captivating to look away.

"The deal was easy to make. But when I returned home there was a sadness that wasn't there when I left. I was told you died. I knew immediately it was punishment for making the deal with Varwik. I also knew I couldn't stay. I didn't pack a thing, didn't say goodbye, I just left. I've spent the years since living with what I had done."

"Then why were you so mean when we met?"

He didn't even pause before answering. "Guilt. I didn't know how to handle seeing you face-to-face. I wasn't sure I believed you really were alive at first, but then I saw you. I saw how beautiful you are. All the anger I felt at Azura over what she did melted away."

"She saved my life."

Oren nodded. "I know. I thought if I turned you away and remained hidden, that Varwik would leave you alone. But then I realized how our meeting must have seemed to you, which is why I'm here today."

"Varwik is forcing me to marry his son."

Oren flinched. "I heard. Oleander, I know I can't change the past, but I will fix the future for you. I will make it right."

"How?" I snapped irritably. I'd been agonizing over how to break the promise for months.

"I'm not sure yet."

I rolled my eyes.

"Look, I wanted you to know how sorry I am. I'm sorry for all the pain I've caused you. I'm sorry for treating you rotten when we met. And I will make it up to you." There was true sadness in Oren's voice.

Plus, a faery couldn't lie. Not even one who'd lived in the human world for sixteen years.

I wasn't sure what to say, so I chose, "Okay."

Oren clasped his hands behind his back, his wings flapping once. "Are you...happy, Oleander?"

"For what it's worth, yes. My human life has been wonderful." I pursed my lips. "It wasn't until this past year that things began falling apart. My life isn't my own anymore."

"You should be allowed to choose your own life, and I will make sure that happens. I promise that."

"You shouldn't make promises," I said wryly. "Then you're expected to keep them."

Oren chuckled. He took my hand in his and kissed it, and in the blink of an eye, he was gone.

Not even a full minute passed before Kallan appeared from the trees, his long legs hurrying across the vivid green grass. He stomped up the stairs, his turquoise eyes surveying the yard. "I heard you had a visitor."

I sighed. "Are there no secrets in the faery world?"

Kallan ignored me. His face was thunderous, and his hands were clenched into fists. "Did he hurt you? I'll kill him if he did anything to cause you more pain."

I knew he meant what he said. Kallan would do anything to protect me.

"No. I'm fine. Oren came to apologize."

Kallan's eyes widened in surprise, and he sank to the wooden swing beside me. "Wow. You okay?"

His leg brushed mine, and I shivered.

"Yeah. Sorry I don't need rescuing this time."

Kallan put his hand on mine. "If you need me for anything, call me and I'll be there. Even if it's just to talk."

"Thanks. You've been so good to me."

"I just want you to be happy. You've been through enough to last a lifetime."

"I'm okay. Really. But I do have a question."

"Of course."

"What's dark magick like?" It had been weighing on my mind, just on the edge of my consciousness, ever since my life had been turned upside down because of it. I regretted asking the second I saw his face.

Kallan's face darkened. "You stay far away from that."

"Why? What's the big fuss about?"

"Nothing worth a fuss at all." His fingers slid into my hair as he tucked it behind my ear. "You are pure, Rylie. Stay that way."

Before I could answer, Kallan kissed my cheek and left.

I was on sensory overload. First Oren, then Kallan. I had so many faery men, all expecting so much from me.

I stared up at the moon just rising in the early evening sky. Dark magick. What was it all about? Could it really have helped Oren find a new power?

I wished I knew more about magick in general. It was still a foreign concept to me, even though I had witnessed magick over and over in the faery world. All I knew was that along with dark magick came power. Obviously, Oren thought the power was worth enough to give me away. His own daughter.

With my power being the ability to use the powers of other faeries, I could access dark magick if I really wanted. It couldn't hurt to learn what dark magick could do. I shook my head. What was I thinking? Dark magick was what separated my birth parents and got me into this mess; why would I want to know anything about it?

On the table next to me, my phone vibrated. The sound was so alien in my thoughts that I shrieked and jumped. I glanced at the screen—Azura.

"Oleander, your cousins are on their way to your house with a gift. Are you home?"

I glanced towards the forest, expecting Nessa and Violet to emerge from the shadowy forest. "Yeah, I'm outside actually. Azura, something happened."

"Oh, good. Your cousins should be there shortly. What happened?"

"Oren showed up."

"Oh dear. Oh, Oleander. Are you all right?"

"He apologized to me. For everything."

Azura's voice was hard when she spoke again. "I suppose he thought that made everything right again."

"I don't think so. He was really sincere."

Her sigh echoed in my ear. "Well, I suppose it's a start."

"Now if only we could find a way out of my promise to Varwik." I caught sight of Nessa and Violet. "Azura, I have to go, they're here."

"Okay, dear. Call me later."

I met my cousins at the top of the stairs, and Nessa handed over a basket.

"What's this?" I asked, raising an eyebrow.

"Fruit for your friend. Have her eat it, and she'll be blessed with faery sight. You'll be able to bring her to our world."

"Really? All she has to do is eat this?" I looked down at the innocuous orange fruit inside. One round piece on a bed of satiny cloth. I felt like the queen in *Snow White* with her apple. At least this fruit wasn't poisoned. I hoped.

Violet nodded. "The fruit is spelled. There are a

couple things to know. One, she has to eat it within the next twenty-four hours. Two, she has to eat it all."

"Got it." I placed the basket on the porch and smiled gratefully. "Thank you both very much."

I was already dialing Sierra's number as my cousins walked away.

CHAPTER TWENTY-THREE

"Okay, I've been dying from the suspense," Sierra said as she pounded up the steps to my porch twenty minutes later. "What on earth was so incredible that you couldn't tell me by phone?"

I let the silence drag, using one foot to slowly swing in the breeze.

She glared at me. "Ry. You're killing me."

Laughing, I said, "Do you still want to go to the faery realm?"

Sierra's mouth dropped open. "Duh!"

"Are you sure? You can still back out."

"I really want to go."

"You can't tell anyone. You can't talk about it. These faeries are trusting you with their lives." I paused. "They're trusting me."

"I would never do anything to hurt you, Ry. Or them."

"I know." I took the fruit out of the basket and held it out. "You have to eat all of it."

"We're going now?" Sierra squeaked, a sudden thread of worry in her voice.

I nodded. I'd already called and told my parents. "Get to it."

She glanced at the fruit still in my hand. "Nothing weird will happen to me, will it?"

"I honestly have no idea. I think it just gives you the ability to see faeries and their world." I also wasn't sure how long it would last, whether the twenty-four hours was faery time or human time.

Carefully, Sierra took the fruit and bit into it. "It's delicious."

"Most faery food is."

"You must love that."

I laughed. "Yeah. It's a plus."

She polished it off and wiped the juice on her jeans. "Now what?"

"I don't know." I poured myself a glass of water.

"You told me before that you used something to hide your faery features from everybody?"

"Yes. Glamour."

"You're using it now?"

"Yes. Why?"

She giggled, her eyes focused over my shoulder. "I can see your wings."

"Then it must be working." I tucked my cell phone in my pocket and left *The Great Gatsby* on the swing. "Ready to take a trip?"

"Nothing looks different," Sierra said as we crossed the tree line and into the forest.

The woods ensconced us completely. The sun was well on its way down, casting everything around us in purple shadows. I was following my instincts towards the faery world, pretty proud of myself because I was certain we were going in the right direction. If it weren't for the warm, breeze-like sensation of the alternate world ahead, I might have been scared of the growing dark.

"I mean, come on, I thought trees, like, glowed with faery dust or something."

I laughed. "We haven't crossed over yet. Be patient."

She looked at me, her eyes squinting through the dim light. "I barely recognize you."

I blushed. There was nothing I could do about it. I couldn't hide from her now. "Does it bother you?"

"No! It's cool. Wait, wait." She halted and held out her hands, her gaze flitting to my wings. "Can I touch them?"

I knew why she wanted to. What human wouldn't? But the thought of someone touching my wings felt so intimate. Like I could say no to my best friend. "Sure."

Sierra reached around me and gently grasped the tips of my wings, then ran her hands all the way down.

My body tingled, and I shivered.

"Can you feel it?" she asked, eyes wide.

"Yeah. It feels good."

"So soft," she said, awe in her voice. "Can you fly?"

I shook my head. "No."

"Lame. What's the point in having wings if you can't fly?"

"I've wondered the same thing myself," I said with a shrug. "Come on. We're almost there."

When we got to what I had started calling the "border," I sensed it by the weird feeling in the pit of my stomach. I stopped and held a hand out to Sierra. "Hold on tight."

"What happens now?" she asked.

"This might feel a little funny."

She giggled nervously. "Okay."

Sierra's grip strengthened as we passed the veil. The usual sensation of upside-down and spinning grabbed hold of me and I briefly closed my eyes to get my bearings. Beside me, Sierra's breathing sped up.

On the other side, I dropped her hand and let her catch her breath for a minute. The panic on her face slowly faded, and I asked, "You okay? It's kinda freaky at first."

"Yeah. That was weird."

"Don't worry." I squeezed her hand. "That was the only really weird thing you'll go through. Well... besides the fact that you'll be surrounded by faeries."

She smiled and her shoulders relaxed. "Then I think I'm gonna be fine."

The sun shone high and hot as we broke through the trees into the field behind Azura's house. I glanced from the corner of my eye and watched Sierra's face brighten. She looked like a kid on Christmas morning.

"This is amazing," she whispered. "Beautiful. The sky is so vivid!"

I remembered my first few times in the faery world and how vibrant the colors had seemed at first. It was kind of ironic that I barely knew anything about this place, yet I couldn't wait to give her a tour. I only knew my way around a small part of the fey world. I secretly hoped to one day know every inch of it.

Azura met us at the door as if she'd sensed us coming. She smiled sweetly at Sierra. "Welcome."

I felt awkward for a moment. I'd shared everything with Sierra since I came clean about my heritage, but this was it. She was meeting my faery mom and, at the moment, staring stupidly up at the tree house.

"Sierra," I said, chuckling.

She whipped her head down. "Yes, yes, sorry. It's just...so cool."

"This is Azura, my...mother."

"Oh! Nice to meet you." Sierra shook Azura's hand. "Thank you for letting me come."

"You're welcome." Azura clasped her hands in front of her silky white dress and gave Sierra a stern look. "As you know, you can never tell anyone about this."

Sierra crossed her heart. "I would never do anything that could hurt Rylie."

Azura inclined her head elegantly. "I believe you. Please, come in."

I let Sierra go first, dying to see her face as she took in the tree house. She gasped, her hands cupping her face. "I can't believe it's all in a tree!"

"I know, right!" I laughed. "It's like something out of a movie."

"Or a dream," Sierra said softly, touching the knotted walls.

"Oleander, why don't you show your friend around the house?" Azura suggested. "I'm making a salad and fresh-baked bread for dinner."

"That sounds great, Azura. Thanks."

As she disappeared to the kitchen, Sierra looked at me and waggled her eyebrows. "Oleander?"

I shushed her, though I laughed, too. "It's my faery name. Azura picked it. Don't make fun."

I led her up the spiral staircase, down the dark hallway that smelled of earth and growing things, and into my room.

"Wow!" Sierra said with an appreciative nod. "This is so you."

"Azura put a lot of thought into decorating."

"She cares about you."

Sierra's absent-minded words sent a pang through me. "I know."

I led her back down the hall as she peeked into the extra bedroom and Azura's, and then we sailed through the kitchen and out the back door. Sierra ooh'd over Azura's gardens, stopping to smell and touch the flowers so many times it made me laugh.

"You act like we don't have flowers back home," I accused her.

"Well, sure, but look at this place, Ry." She threw out her arms and spun in a circle. "It's like paradise. Breathtaking!"

I could only nod. I'd thought the same thing myself.

We ventured out to the common area inside the circle of tree houses. I'd noticed before all the dirt roads leading away from the village, and I assumed there was much more to the light faery world than just this small neighborhood, but I'd yet to go exploring. I was almost too nervous to leave the safety of Azura's company.

"It's so hard to leave sometimes," I spoke up as we passed a group of older chatting women. I made a beeline for an empty picnic table.

As we sat down, Sierra asked, "Then why do you leave? You have a room, and Azura obviously loves you and would take care of you."

I made a "duh" face. "My parents, Adam, you."

"You could still come visit, right?"

I burst out laughing. Here was my best friend in the whole world telling me I should stay in a completely separate dimension from her. "I mean, don't you want me around?" I teased.

She shoved me gently. "Of course I do. But this place is beyond words. How could you not want to be here?" She sighed. "Maybe it's just because my home life sucks so much. It's not that I don't love my family, but it's so hard. You don't have siblings or a nephew bugging you, parents nagging you to help out, and a horrible love life."

She had a point. If I'd had her life, I would have probably wanted to stay with Azura.

Sierra pointed at the cloud of piskies dancing over my aunt's vegetable garden. "What are those? Tiny faeries?"

"Piskies," I corrected. "They're another faery-type creature. Don't watch them too long, and definitely don't let them convince you to follow them into the trees."

"Why?"

"They'll make you feel wonderful, then they'll make you dance until you forgot who you are and where you're from."

Sierra looked stricken. "But...everything here isn't good?"

"It isn't that they're bad," I said, my gaze shifting back to the piskies. They flitted well above the garden, chattering as the sun shone off their colorful backs. I laughed. "They just have a purpose that's counterproductive to ours."

When she didn't respond, I looked back at her, puzzled to find she was staring at something. I followed her gaze to a crowd of faeries roughly our age, or at least appearing to be our age. I recognized several boys I'd met at the spring festival, one of whom was staring right back at Sierra.

"Earth to Sierra." I waved my hand in front of her face.

"He's gorgeous," she responded without tearing her gaze from the now-smiling faery guy.

I smirked. "I didn't ask."

"Who is he?"

Squinting in his direction, I tried to recall his name. "I have no idea. I've met him before, but I can't remember."

Before I finished speaking, the guy started our way, shoving his hands into the pockets of his blue jeans.

"Oh my God," Sierra breathed. "Oh my God, Ry, he's coming over. Do I look okay?"

As she whipped towards me, she almost fell off the bench. She teetered on the edge, hands flailing, and I reached out and caught her arms. "Chill. You look fine. Deep breaths."

My best friend attempted to play it cool, but I knew she was sweating by the time he drew up beside us.

"Hey, Oleander." He was darkly good-looking with shaggy brown hair and tanned skin. He flashed a bright smile in Sierra's direction. "Who's this?"

"Please call me Rylie." I sighed. I didn't mind Azura and her family calling me that, but I really didn't want it to stick. "This is Sierra."

He stuck out a hand. "I'm Drake."

"Hi, Drake."

If my best friend's mouth hung open any more, she'd be drooling.

"You are positively enchanting," Drake said. Neither of them had taken their eyes from each other.

I rolled my eyes. Seriously? I bring my friend to the faery world and she finds a guy. Not just any guy, a faery. Only Sierra.

"So, you're O—" Drake glanced at me. "Rylie's friend?"

"Best friend." She blushed.

"Why don't you have a seat?" I motioned to the bench next to Sierra.

He didn't have to be told twice. Folding his long, lanky body down right beside her, he said, "So Sierra—you're human."

Sierra laughed. "And, Drake...you're a faery."

They fell into easy conversation, doing the usual rounds of getting to know one another. I tried to fade into the background so I wouldn't intrude. Things had been so rough for Sierra this year. She needed some small measure of happiness, and in just five minutes of Drake's presence, her face had brightened so much.

The clatter of cart wheels and the low murmur of people drifted to us from the small market across the village. The market consisted of wooden shacks built close together, protecting a wide variety of goods from vegetables to textiles to books. What made it lovely were the sparkling lights hanging from the eaves of the huts, and the way the browsing faeries weaved in and out. When Sierra was done flirting, we had to walk over there.

I'd never seen anything like that open-air market back in the human world. Living here would be pretty awesome. If only I could have the best of both worlds...but why couldn't I? Could I make it work? Like a joint-custody arrangement. I only had one more year of school, and it was really important to my parents that I graduate. It was important to me, too. After that, what would keep me from spending my time between both worlds?

I noticed Violet and Nessa walking down the trail with canvas bags hanging off their arms, coming from the direction of the market. I figured Sierra was safe with Drake, so I hustled over to see my cousins.

"Oleander! You made it." Violet grinned, switching her bag from one arm to the other. "We just finished shopping for dinner."

"Mom's making my favorite casserole," Nessa said happily.

"Is that your human friend?" Violet squinted at Sierra and Drake still conversing as if I'd not even left. Her eyebrows furrowed. "She's talking to Drake. What's going on there?"

I shrugged. "Puppy love?"

"Love? Between a faery and a human?" My cousins exchanged glances.

"Why not?" I asked.

Violet shrugged. "It doesn't happen."

"Ever?" I knew that wasn't true. After all, I'd fallen in love with Adam.

"Rarely."

I didn't like where this conversation was going. Crossing my arms over my chest, I asked, "Have a faery and a human ever married?"

"I've heard of it, but it never ends well." Violet looked at Sierra and Drake and shook her head. "Faeries should be with faeries."

"Why?" I pushed. "Why can't faeries choose what they want?"

"My mom says it's against nature," Nessa spoke up. I'd almost forgotten she was there, she was so silent.

I bit back a sharp retort and settled for a subtle nudge. "So my relationship with my human boyfriend is against nature. Funny how right it feels."

Both girls looked chagrined.

"Is it illegal?"

"No. It's not against our laws," Violet assured me. "It's just... It's not looked upon favorably."

"Things in your world need to change."

"Change isn't easy." Violet shifted on her feet.

"No, but it's inevitable." I pointed at Sierra and Drake. "Look at them. They have an instant connection. How can you tell them this isn't right?"

"Look, I know this is about you and your human boyfriend," Violet started.

"Adam. His name is Adam."

"Adam," she relented. "But Oleander, you've never even been with a faery. How do you know what you're missing?"

Violet's words haunted me long after they were gone.

CHAPTER TWENTY-FOUR

I finally managed to drag my best friend away from her new beau—with a promise we would see him in the morning.

All the way back to Azura's, she couldn't stop talking about him. "Did you know he lives right next door to your cousins? And he's in this progressive school where they learn outside and there's only five people in his class. Oh, and he plays the harp, how cool is that? Who plays a harp anymore?"

I chuckled. She had it bad.

"Drake is perfect."

"You hardly know him."

"There's just something about him. Haven't you felt that way?"

I groaned. "Yeah. Twice."

"I keep forgetting about Kallan. Ry, if you chose to be with him, you could be here. Forever." Sierra motioned to our surroundings, to Azura's tree house growing shadowed as the sun set, the windows warmly glowing. "Don't you love it here?"

"I do."

"And you love Kallan," Sierra said gently.

"I don't know how I feel about Kallan."

"That usually means love."

I punched her on the shoulder. "Come on. Azura is going to have dinner waiting."

As we mounted the steps to the porch, Sierra spoke again. "Do you think it could work with him?"

I raised an eyebrow. "Me and Kallan?"

Rolling her eyes, Sierra shoved me. "No, you idiot, me and Drake."

"I have no idea. I guess it could work if you really want it to." I decided not to tell her about my conversation with Nessa and Violet earlier. People had a tendency to be obstacles to themselves. It wouldn't help her any to feel like she'd failed before she even tried.

Sierra's face smoothed into a dreamy look. "It would be so neat to be loved by a faery."

"You already are. By me."

She hit my shoulder. "I love you, too. Thanks for this."

"It's not over yet. Wait 'til you eat dinner!"

After a delicious dinner, during which conversation with Azura flowed easily, I showed Sierra to the extra bedroom.

It was smaller than mine, but cozy, with white bedcovers and a large window overlooking the backyard. I checked to make sure there were sheets on the bed and showed her where the bathroom was.

"I can see the garden in the faery lights," Sierra breathed, looking outside.

"This place always seems to be full of twinkling lights."

"Like a wonderland."

I laughed. "Yeah. Every time I come, I feel like Alice down the rabbit hole."

We stared at each other across the bedroom for a moment, sharing happy smiles.

"Ry, this has been...I don't know. Amazing, spectacular, stupendous." Sierra giggled. "All those adjectives and more. Thank you."

I nodded. "I'm just across the hall if you need me."

"Are you sure it's okay to stay? I mean, shouldn't I call my mom?"

I shook my head. "Remember, time is weird here. She won't even know you were gone."

In my room, I checked my phone—by habit; it wasn't like I'd have any messages in another dimension—and then crawled into bed. With the way my emotions had been in turmoil from Oren's appearance until now, I was asleep almost instantly.

When I awoke, it was pitch black outside and the house was quiet. I stared up at the shadows moving on my ceiling, wondering what it was that had jarred me from sleep.

Then it came again. A tap-tap-tap at the window.

I shoved the covers off and crossed to the window, pushing aside the curtains.

Kallan.

He was illuminated in the front yard by the moon. Silvery light shone off his satin hair as he threw another small pebble at the glass.

How in the world did he know where my room was?

I didn't bother with shoes. I made my silent way through the house, past Sierra's closed door and

Azura's open one. I could see my faery mother's form in bed, her platinum hair spread across her pillow.

The stairs were quiet, thankfully, and so was the front door as I pulled it open.

"What are you doing here?" I hissed, coming to a stop before Kallan.

He looked rumpled, his dark hair a mussed halo above his head and his T-shirt and jeans wrinkled as if he'd picked them up off the floor. I couldn't remember ever seeing him so not put together.

"Checking on you," he said softly. He cleared his throat. "You disappeared."

"Like you don't?" I retorted. "How did you know what room I was in?"

He smiled playfully. "A little piskie told me."

I felt the tension leave my body and the corners of my mouth turned up just a bit. "Why are you here, Kallan?"

He shrugged. "I worry."

"You don't have to worry about me. It's sweet, but I'm fine."

"I couldn't stop it if I tried." He shook his head. "I have this overwhelming urge to protect you. I haven't seen you too much since we got back from...vacation."

"How did you even get here? I thought dark faeries had to be invited in."

Kallan looked down at the ground. "There was a faery near the border. I used mind control on him to get him to invite me in."

"Kallan!" I couldn't help but laugh. Kallan took a step closer and my pulse raced. We weren't even touching, but I could feel electricity between us. I bit down on my lip, wanting him to make a move and knowing how wrong I was for wanting it. I desperately wanted to feel his lips on mine.

Before he could say anything else, the steady pit-pat of feet on dirt interrupted us. I froze, suddenly realizing that I was standing in front of Azura's house with the prince of the dark faery world, and we were about to be caught.

It was my aunt. Her long blonde hair, the same sheen as Azura's, was pulled into a messy braid, and she had pillowcase creases on her cheek beneath sleepy eyes.

"Oleander!" she gasped, grabbing my arm.

"I'm fine! He's safe, he isn't going to hurt me!" I said quickly, angling to put myself in front of Kallan.

Lorella shook her head. "No, Oleander. I am not here about the dark prince."

"What is it?"

"Your friend. The human."

As my aunt's hand fell away from my arm, I asked, "Sierra?"

Lorella held out a hand, her face softening. "Yes! Sierra is in trouble!"

I didn't pause to see if she or Kallan would follow me. I raced for the tree house and shoved open the door, taking the stairs two at a time. Skidding to a halt in front of Sierra's room, I turned the knob.

Locked.

"Back away." Kallan's voice was hard.

I didn't question how awkward it was for him to be in my mother's house. I sidestepped and watched as he took hold of the knob and slammed his shoulder into the door.

Azura called my name just as the door gave way beneath Kallan. He stumbled into the room with me hot on his heels, while Lorella spoke softly to her sister.

Sierra's bed was mussed, the curtains on her window swaying in the breeze.

Sierra was gone.

CHAPTER TWENTY-FIVE

"What do you know?" I demanded of Lorella, my hands balling into fists at my side.

Kallan put a gentle hand on my shoulder and squeezed, showing his solidarity.

My aunt stood beside Azura, the two so similar in the dark hallway it was like seeing double. They both even wore the same type of gauzy, full-length nightgown.

Azura grimaced. "Sweetie, calm down."

"She snuck out of the house," Lorella murmured.

"Why?" I clenched my fists, horrified that my best friend had betrayed my trust. I'd brought her to the faery world because she begged me, and now she'd run off in the middle of the night.

Lorella grimaced. "To meet a boy."

I groaned. "Drake."

Her eyes took on a faraway gaze, as if she were

looking inside herself. "She wandered into neutral territory."

Kallan cursed.

He obviously knew something I didn't. "What happened to her?" I asked, my voice screechy.

"She was found by goblins."

I glared at Kallan. "And?"

He grimaced. "It isn't the first time they've taken someone. Which means my father now has a human."

"Is she okay?" I asked Lorella.

"Yes. For now. Varwik does not know his goblins have her."

"It's only a matter of time," Kallan said darkly.

"Then we go get her." I headed for my room to get dressed.

"No, Rylie, you will stay here," Kallan said, following me into my room. "I will retrieve your friend."

"You're crazy," I told him with a shrug, yanking my jeans off the footboard of the bed. "I'm going. She's my best friend."

"Ry..." Kallan came closer and took my hand, blue jeans dangling from the other. "I don't want you anywhere near my father or the dark territory."

"Why?" I unfolded my jeans and kicked off my shoes. "I'm not obligated to honor the promise until next year. He has no sway over me."

"Please. Let me take care of Sierra. I don't want to risk anything happening to you."

I paused only for a moment. "Get out, Kallan. I'm changing, and then we're going. We'll figure out the rest when we get there."

As soon as I stepped out into the night, I saw Azura ready to go. Oh no. That wasn't happening. With Kallan nearby, I stood in front of Azura and using Kallan's mind control I told her, "You will stay here with Lorella."

Kallan raised his eyebrows in surprise.

"I might be able to help."

"I have Kallan to help me. I'll be fine, please just wait here for me."

My mother sighed and nodded. "I'll wait for you here."

Not like she had a choice.

"Thank you." I didn't want Azura around Varwik. Not that I thought he would hurt her. I kind of thought she would hurt him. And as much as I wouldn't have minded seeing her punch his lights out, my faery mother was a little sweeter than that. I didn't want her to do anything she would regret.

Kallan and I began walking. "Using my mind control again, huh?"

"I have enough to worry about without having to worry about her," I said through clenched teeth.

Though I had a feeling I was going to regret my decision to go.

The woods were darker and more menacing with the sky so black. The moon filtered through the thick canopy of trees overhead, giving us only a little light to see by, but Kallan seemed to know where he was going.

"How do you know your way around here?" I asked him, taking his hand as he helped me over a fallen tree. The branches were cracked and broken. I wondered if it'd fallen because of goblins.

"All faeries have an internal compass of sorts." Kallan held back branches on a particularly thick bramble bush so that I could slide through.

That's right. Azura had explained that to me. I guess I just didn't realize it worked on both sides. I still had so much to learn.

"Kallan!" The voice cut through the darkness like a gunshot.

I jumped and grabbed onto Kallan, putting him between the voice and me like some scared little girl.

"It's okay," Kallan rushed to assure me, his warm arm sliding around my shoulder. "I know that voice. He's a friend."

The darkness parted to reveal a dark-haired faery with black and blue wings. He nodded to me and then turned his gaze to Kallan with a bow of his head. "My prince."

"What's going on, Tiern?"

"Oren."

The one word fell between us, putting me on edge immediately.

Kallan swore under his breath. "Is he..."

Horrified, I realized Kallan was asking if my father was dead.

Tiern shook his head. "No, but Lord Varwik intends to remedy that."

Kallan turned his back on Tiern and took me by the arms. "Rylie, please. Go home. Go back to the human world. This is going to get messy fast."

"You're naive if you think I'm not coming. He's my father."

He scoffed, and gave Tiern a pointed look. "You're naive if you think you are."

Behind Kallan, Tiern clapped his hands. There was a flash of light so blinding that I lost my ability to see. I reached for Kallan, but my fingertips only touched air. By the time my vision returned, they were gone.

Jerk.

Nothing pissed me off more than a guy thinking

he needed to protect me. I'd been held captive by his own people for weeks. If I couldn't handle a little fight, then what kind of faery was I?

I spun around in a circle, trying to get my bearings. When it came to getting to the faery world, I'd gotten that down. But finding the dark side was a whole different story. I hadn't been there in over a year. Which way was it? I closed my eyes and took a few deep breaths. My heart felt like it was being pulled in one direction. That was the way I'd go.

I snapped open my eyes and took off in the direction that felt right. Every snap of a twig beneath my feet terrified me, echoing in the forest as if it came from somewhere else. I rushed forward, swiping my hair out of my face and keeping my eyes on my surroundings.

When a hand clamped onto my shoulder, I shrieked loud enough to startle birds from their perches.

I tore from the grasp and swiveled around, landing on my butt with all the grace of a baby goat.

I stared up, bewildered. I recognized the face looking down at me. "Drake!"

He offered a hand. "Sorry, Rylie. I didn't mean to frighten you."

"How did you find me?"

He heaved me to my feet. "Azura and Lorella sent me."

"Why?"

"Lorella saw Kallan would leave you when word came of your father. I'm 'backup,' I believe she said." He grimaced. "Besides, it's my fault Sierra is in this mess. She was coming to meet me."

"Well, remind me to thank Lorella." I brushed leaves and dirt off the seat of my pants. "Do you know the way to the dark territory?"

"I do."

"Did they tell you..." I trailed off.

"About Sierra?" His jaw clenched. "Yes. We will save her."

I nodded. "All right then. Lead the way."

When we crossed the border, the woods changed. The sun was beginning to rise, bathing the forest in the gray glow of dawn. Drake put a finger to his lips and looked away. I followed his gaze, focusing on the sounds of the forest.

Voices.

"What is that?"

"Our destination, I'd wager." His dark eyes caught mine. "Let's go invisible, Rylie. We don't want to be seen walking up."

He had a point. We weren't positive exactly what we were walking in to, and if we came in invisible, we'd have the advantage.

I recognized the castle the moment we left the trees behind. It rose before us, black-stoned and thunderous. I couldn't locate the source of the shouting, but it seemed to be coming from around back. Still invisible, we entered the cold shadow of the castle.

I just hoped I wasn't about to find my father dead.

CHAPTER TWENTY-SIX

Oren stood ten feet from Varwik with his sword drawn. Two armed guards were between them, both with swords out and pointed at Oren.

To the left, Kallan stood with his hands out like he was a cop showing he was unarmed.

At least everybody was still breathing.

"Find Sierra," I whispered to Drake, even though I couldn't see him. "Try the castle. When they had me imprisoned, I was kept there." I gave him a brief description of how to get to the room where I'd been held.

"I will find her. Stay safe."

I felt his presence move away, and I was alone.

Varwik had barely changed at all since the last time I saw him. His black hair was a bit shorter, and he still had a goatee that wouldn't have looked out of place on a movie villain. His black and purple wings stood tall and proud behind him.

"Are we going to do this all day, Varwik?" Oren

said, his voice loud. "Why don't you come face me yourself instead of hiding behind your guards? This is between us. Not the guards, not our kids."

Varwik's eyes narrowed. Taking the challenge, he waved away his guards and stepped forward as they parted. "Very well, Oren. Now what? Do you really think you can kill me? I have no weapon in my hands. That would disgrace you."

"You think I care? I've already been disgraced."

"I think we both know you don't stand a chance against me, flower boy."

Ignoring the barb, Oren spoke again. "I will spare your life if you release my daughter from her promise. Let her enjoy life the way she wants."

Panic filled me. This was over me. My father would take on the most powerful dark faery with just his weak power, and all for me. I was flooded with warmth. Too bad his grand, heroic gesture was almost seventeen years too late.

Varwik laughed. "Tough talk for such a weak man."

"I've been training the last sixteen years for this moment."

"You'd need more than sixteen years." Varwik bowed ironically. "Do you forget who I am?"

"I know exactly who you are. If anyone is weak, it's you. Forcing a girl to marry your son. Pathetic."

"She's an Aurorian," he said simply. "I need her on my side. I need her power."

"She'd rather die than help you." Oren pointed his sword at Varwik.

"How would you know? You abandoned her. All I'm asking is for her to marry my son so she can't use her powers against us. I have no plan to cause her harm. It's a fair deal."

"For now!" Oren snarled. "You'll come up with something else when it suits you. I won't let you have that kind of hold on her. You're right, I wasn't there for her growing up, but I will be there now when she needs me."

"How sweet, but you have no choice. We made a deal years ago. Now that I have her, you can have the access to dark magick. Why don't you take it and go back to wherever it is you've been hiding for the past sixteen years?"

"Keep your dark magick. I was a fool. I just want peace for my daughter."

"She will marry my son. She will do what I say or her family will be killed. As you know, a deal promise cannot be broken."

Branches crunched beneath my feet as I took a few steps closer. Oren was trying to break the promise. He truly cared about me and wanted me safe. So when he'd promised me he would find a way, he'd meant it. But looking at Varwik now, I couldn't see it happening.

Varwik didn't care. He was cold and heartless.

"Let her go. You can have me," Oren said bravely.

"You're pathetic. What would I want with you? So you could tell me what flowers smell good?" Varwik smirked.

"This is your last chance. Give my daughter her freedom."

"This should be fun." Varwik extended his arm and, without prompting, one of the guards placed a sword in his hand. He gripped the hilt of the dangerously sharp blade and faced Oren.

Not another word passed between them before Varwik attacked.

Their swords clanged as they came together time

and time again. Both men were well-trained fighters, and it showed. They stepped around an imaginary circle, trading thrusts with a speed I had a hard time following. My father had no trouble matching Varwik.

"I've underestimated you," Varwik grunted with a hint of admiration in his voice.

"I told you I've been practicing," Oren said coldly, deflecting a heavy blow away from his shoulder with ease. "I've had a lot of free time on my hands. You took everything from me."

"You accepted the deal." Clank, clank.

I glanced at Kallan, wondering why he wasn't doing anything. He could have at least tried to stop them or yelled. Why was he just standing there? He seemed to be hypnotized by the swinging of the swords.

It dawned on me that he could use his mind control—not that it would do much with Varwik being immune to all other faery powers. I thought about using his mind control. I was close enough, but I wouldn't be able to stop Varwik, only Oren. Instead, I held back and waited.

Varwik lunged forward, his sword stopping only inches from Oren's neck as my father managed to get his blade between them and thrust the blow away. Oren stumbled, but only for a second before his boots were again grinding in the dirt. He was breathing heavy, gasping for air as sweat trickled down his face.

"Done yet?" Varwik asked. "I'll even be a good sport and not hold this little fight against you."

Oren's knuckles turned white as he gripped his sword tighter. "I will forever be ashamed of what I did. I will make it up to her. This is the only way I know how, even if it costs me my life."

Varwik laughed. "How noble of you."

"She's my daughter," Oren responded with a

new vengeance, sweat dripping from his head. Their swords met again, and Varwik's moves seemed faster and stronger. Oren was forced backwards.

It was clear to me that neither one of them were going to give in, and with my father's most recent declaration of love for me, I had to do something. I had to end this fight.

"Stop!" I yelled, letting myself become visible as I jumped into the fray.

I felt icy power course through my veins. The ground began to rumble beneath my feet. It was as if my whole body radiated and I was drunk with power.

"Rylie, no!" Kallan yelled.

Both men's faces registered shock, but they were moving too fast, and I appeared too suddenly. I wasn't sure who hit me or how, but stars burst in my vision and pain blossomed in my head. I hit the ground, dazed, my vision swimming.

My father screamed, and a blur leapt over me that I assumed was Oren. Another crash of metal, and then Kallan's deep voice. Another blur—this one of turquoise wings—and then grunting.

I wanted to lift my hand, to call for Kallan and keep him from doing the stupid thing I'd done by jumping between the two men. Oren and Varwik were out for blood.

"Father! Stop!" Kallan yelled, and then I heard an "Oof!" and he fell next to me.

Had Varwik hit his own son?

The power that had just filled every nerve ending in my body was gone. I was left feeling empty and scared and I didn't understand. I tried to focus on Kallan, but my vision was still spinning. By the lack of sound but steady breathing, I surmised he'd been knocked out.

I managed to turn shakily and get my hands and knees beneath me. I thought I croaked Oren's name, and I might have called him Dad. By the time I lifted my gaze to the two fighting men, the battle had reached its climax.

In a moment of arrogance, Varwik lifted his sword high and sneered, "You'll never beat me, you weak, pathetic man."

Oren, bloodied, bruised, and beaten, saw an opening. In a clean, swift movement, his sword passed through Varwik's body.

Shocked, Varwik gasped. But I could tell, even through the dizziness, that it wasn't over. I screamed Oren's name as Varwik's sword came down on his neck.

Oren gasped and his hand flew to the side of his neck. Dark red liquid flowed through his fingers, quicker than blood should have flowed from a wound. I knew it was fatal.

Varwik fell first. Oren swayed over him for a moment. Then almost as if in slow motion, my father fell to the ground beside the dark faery.

"No!" I shrieked. With a rush of new energy, I scrambled on all fours to his side. Blood pulsed from his wound. I tried putting pressure on it, but it coated my hands in seconds.

Our eyes met and even though he was breathing hard, he smiled. "My daughter... It will be okay. This was meant to be. The promise is broken now."

Reality hit me hard. If Varwik died, the deal he made with my father was void—as was his deal with me. If just Oren died, my promise to Varwik would be upheld. I was too powerful for him to let go. I was sure of that. But if he died, I'd be free.

As I looked into Oren's eyes, I found myself wondering if being free was worth the cost. He had killed Varwik, but would give his own life in doing so. I would never know the man who helped bring me into this world.

"Don't die..." I begged softly.

"Death is a blessing." He didn't say anything else, maybe because he didn't have the energy or he thought I wouldn't want to hear it. Or maybe because he knew I could see the love in his eyes. With a smile on his face, he closed his eyes and took his last breath.

In the silence that followed, I heard footsteps rushing towards me. Still woozy from my head wound, I glanced up, looking for the source.

Lena.

The pale, blonde faery paused, her blue eyes assessing the situation. Kallan out cold, Oren and I with hands entwined, and Varwik with a sword standing out of his chest.

I couldn't speak. Hot tears built in my eyes, and the lump in my throat felt immovable.

Lena looked back and forth between Oren and Varwik. I saw the moment she chose her path.

With soft, steady steps, she came to my father and me and knelt beside us.

"Help him. Please." My voice cracked.

Her capable hands drifted over my father's body, and her eyes closed. Magick shimmered off of her in waves as she tried to do what she could for Oren.

At last, she shook her head and sat back on her heels. "I'm so sorry, Oleander. He's already gone. There's nothing I can do."

That wasn't good enough. I was an Aurorian and with Lena here, I could use her power. I placed my hands on my father's neck and willed it to heal. Yanking them back, I was devastated to find the wound still there and Oren still dead.

"We can't bring them back from the dead. We can only heal the living."

"And Varwik?" I asked bitterly, my gaze settling on the leader of the dark faeries.

Lena looked around us. "The guards who came for me have not yet returned. There was a scuffle inside the castle." She smiled wryly. "Varwik's human prisoner is gone."

I let my head fall to the grass and sighed. "Thank God."

Lena glanced at Varwik. "Oleander, you know Varwik has held me against my will at this palace for years."

I nodded. Oren's hand was sticky in mine.

"He threatened to murder my family if I did not serve him." Her blue-eyed gaze caught mine.

I nodded again.

Then I watched, dumbfounded, as Lena climbed gracefully to her feet, crossed to Varwik, and spit on him. She didn't even bother to see if he could be saved.

CHAPTER
TWENTY-SEVEN

By the time Kallan came to beneath Lena's healing hands, Varwik and Oren were both gone. "Maybe this is for the best," Kallan murmured, wiping away a tear from his face.

I didn't answer. Maybe he was right. They did this to themselves, both for their own reasons. Varwik with a thirst for power, and Oren with a determination to save me.

I bent over and kissed Oren's forehead. I didn't know him as my father, but that didn't matter. He was, and always would be.

"Thank you," I whispered into his ear.

Lena and Kallan helped me stand. Though the healer had helped my injury, my equilibrium was still off. It took me a moment to find my feet. When I did, I started walking away.

"Ry?" Kallan's voice was thick with worry.

I stopped in my tracks, tears flowing down my face. I fought the urge to turn around. "I'm done here," I said simply and continued walking.

I had no doubt that my best friend was safe with Drake, nor did I doubt that Lorella had seen the outcome of the fight and dutifully informed Azura. I didn't want to stay in this world any longer than I had to, so I left behind the blood, the devastation, and a guy who loved me, and I went back home.

It was nighttime and every light in the house was on.

I walked in the back door to find my parents, Drake, and Sierra gathered in the kitchen. My parents sat at the table with steaming mugs, while Sierra held an ice pack to a bump on her head. Drake stood at the counter, his arms crossed over his chest.

I looked at each of their worried faces. I had no clue what to say. The enormity of what I'd witnessed sat on my shoulders like a monster I couldn't shake.

"Rylie?" Mom asked gently.

I swallowed hard. "Yeah?"

"What happened?"

"The promise is broken. I no longer have to marry Kallan."

"How?" Dad put a hand on Mom's.

"Varwik and Oren are dead. They killed each other."

"Oh honey..." Mom's hand flew up to her mouth.

I looked at Sierra. "Are you okay?"

"Fine, thanks to Drake." She flashed a weary smile in his direction.

A long silence followed. If I was at a loss for words, it seemed everyone else was too.

I finally spoke again. "I'm finished. I don't want

anything to do with this anymore. I hope you can all understand that."

Before anyone could say anything else, I turned and left.

I closed and locked my bedroom door, and then stood in front of the mirror. I almost didn't recognize myself. Not as a human or a faery. My once happy eyes looked sad. My hair was a mess of dirt and leaves, and probably blood if the sticky substance behind my ear was anything. My hands and legs were dirty. My wings sagged.

I sobbed once and sank down on the edge of my bed. Nothing seemed real. It felt as though I'd been going through the motions lately. I wished I could run away like Oren did for so many years. I'd probably be found eventually...just like he was.

Being a faery was what little girls dreamed of. I should have been happy. Excited. But I wasn't. Miserable was a better word for what this past year had been. I curled up into a ball on my bed. Life hadn't been easy, but maybe now with the faery thing gone, I could concentrate on my human life. School, grades, colleges, and Adam.

Things would go back to normal now...right?

I closed my eyes and let sleep take over.

CHAPTER TWENTY-EIGHT

The birds outside my window started singing extra early the next morning. I yanked the blankets over my head and tried to block their noise. I rolled over on my side and stayed there, tucked inside the covers, all day long. There were plenty of knocks on the door, but I sent them all away. My phone trilled constantly until I finally turned it off.

I couldn't make heads or tails of everything that had happened. I had found my father, he said he didn't want anything to do with me, then he apologized to me, and said he'd make it right. Never in a million years did I think he'd be dead a couple days later. He had faced Varwik for me, to give me my freedom. And what was I doing with it? Spending it in bed. Right now, I was okay with that.

"Rylie?" Mom knocked again.

"I just need sleep," I told her.

The knob turned, and she walked in. "C'mon, Rylie. It's dinnertime. Please come eat."

"I'm not hungry."

She sat at the edge of the bed. "Do you want to talk about it?"

"No."

"Some serious stuff happened. I'm sure you're confused. Dad and I...we're here for you."

"I know."

She sat there for a few more minutes, sighed, and then left. Around midnight, sleepless and with a desperate need for something to distract me, I got up and rearranged my dresser drawers.

I moved on to my closet, starting with the floorboard where my shoes were arranged by size and type. I moved a lamp closer so I could see, and as I dug around in the dusty back corner, I found what I was looking for—a flat, white box with a crushed side.

I pulled it out and traced my name, which was written on top in black marker. Opening the top, I peered inside. A soft pink and brown blanket lay on the top. I took it out and pressed it to my face. My baby blanket. It was worn from years of hugging it, soaking up tears, and being dragged around. I placed it in my lap and looked back in the box.

There were a few pictures and cards that were important to me. A friendship bracelet Sierra had given me years ago. A ribbon I received for winning the spelling bee in elementary school. The box was full of mementos from my life, something I had put together over the years. The contents meant something to me, yet each was something I never would have had if Azura hadn't switched me. It almost felt like they should belong to someone else.

I didn't come out of my room for the next four days other than to use the bathroom. Mom brought me food and sat with me while I ate it. I'm sure it was more for her than for me. She wanted to make sure I was eating something. I definitely wasn't good company. By the end of the third day, I had caught up on all of my schoolwork and gone through everything in my room. I felt somewhat calmer.

On the fifth night, my door swung open and Sierra stalked into the room.

I was on my bed, surrounded by pictures from my childhood. I stared at my best friend, pretty sure the door had been locked.

Sierra pointed at me. "You are not one to sulk. You are a fighter. Now get back up and do something about this mess."

I couldn't look her in the eye, so I glanced back down at the picture in my lap. A school picture. Fourth grade, I thought. "This is different."

"No, it's not, Rylie. Something terrible happened. You have to move past it."

"It's only been like three days!"

"Three days of hiding in your room. You've had time to think. Now it's time to act."

"Act on what? I'm done. Finished. I want to get my grades back up and move on with my life."

"You can't just pretend nothing happened."

"Why not? When did you become queen?"

Sierra looked hurt, and for a second, I felt bad. "I'm just worried about you."

"Really?" The anger grew in me again. "Is this about me or you? You've got a boyfriend now and the only way to keep him is through me, right? Isn't that why you're here? To make sure you don't lose your faery boyfriend?"

She gasped. "Rylie...I...you..." Tears fell down her cheeks. "He has nothing to do with this. I love you, Ry. You're my best friend and you're hurting. I just want to help." She spun on her heel and walked out the door.

I hadn't noticed my parents standing behind her.

"Nice. Real nice," my mom commented sarcastically and followed Sierra.

Dad stood there a moment longer.

"What do you want?" I asked him, my arms folded in front of me.

"I was just thinking of how things used to be. You would never have treated Sierra like that. You wouldn't sulk in your room. So much has happened, and it's changing you. I'm not sure I like it, and there's nothing I can do about it." He sighed and walked away.

I curled up under the covers and sobbed, my tears soaking the pillow. Sierra was right. I needed to stop being such a brat and get over it. Problem was, I didn't know how to do that. I decided right then that I would sulk for the rest of the night and when morning came, I would start anew.

When I woke in the morning, I remembered my decision and jumped into it with zeal. After I took my shower, I dressed in a pair of worn jeans and a violet shirt. I stood in front of the bathroom mirror and stared at myself: pointed ears, wings, and all.

"A new day," I murmured.

I put a smile on my face when I walked into the kitchen. Mom and Dad looked up, both of them astonished to see me out of my room.

"Hey," I said guiltily. In the harsh of light of day, I

felt like a jerk for the way I'd been acting.

"You look...better," Mom said.

I nodded. "Do we have any muffins?"

"Blueberry." Dad pointed to the counter.

I grabbed two out of the package and ate them quickly. "After last night, I don't know if Sierra is going to show up and bring me to school. Do you think one of you might be able to drop me off?"

Mom and Dad exchanged glances, and Dad nodded. "Of course. I'll take you."

I said goodbye to Mom and followed him to the car. We were out of the driveway before he finally spoke.

"Can I say something?" Dad asked.

"Sure." I chewed on my lip and gripped my backpack in my lap, worried about what he would say.

"I love you. No matter who or what you are, I love you."

Relief filled me. That hadn't been what I expected. "Thanks, Dad. I love you, too."

"I just wanted you to know that..." He stumbled over his words. "I've never been a big fan of this faery stuff. I want you home and safe. But I want you to know that whatever you decide, I will support you."

I blinked a few times to keep the tears away. "Thank you."

He pulled up to the school. "Thanks for listening to me babble."

"It means a lot," I said with a shake of my head. "Right now I'm going to concentrate on school and Adam..." My eyes traveled to the front of the school, where Adam was hanging out with his friends.

"Only you can choose your own destiny, Ry. Don't forget that." Dad cupped my face and pressed a kiss to my forehead.

"I love you, Dad." I stepped out of the car, shut the

door, and walked towards Adam.

When he looked up and saw me, he jumped up. "Rylie!" he exclaimed.

I set my bag down and put my arms around his neck. "Hold me?"

"Of course." He put his hand on the small of my back and held me close. Burying his face in my hair, he took a deep breath. "You smell so good. I've missed it."

"I'm sorry. I've been so distracted." I pulled back and looked in his eyes. "That's all over. I'm focused on you and school from now on."

"You ready to tell me what's been going on?"

The bell rang.

"Don't think that lets you off the hook."

I smiled, took his hand, and walked towards the school doors. "We'll talk after school."

"I'm gonna hold you to that."

"I promise."

At the beginning of each of my classes, I spoke with each of my teachers and handed in any back work I had. I even begged a few for extra credit. By the end of the day, my backpack was twice as heavy as when I got to school, but I felt pretty good about it.

Maybe everything I'd been through had shown me exactly what was important.

Sierra was nowhere to be found. I tried texting her, but she didn't answer. Guess she was extremely annoyed with me. I would have to fix that, too.

I met up with Adam at the end of the day. "Can we talk here?" I asked. I didn't want to talk at my house.

"Sure." He took my hand and led me over to a picnic table.

"Remember that lady you met a couple weeks ago?"

"The one with the weird name?"

"Yeah. Azura. Turns out she's my biological mother."

Adam's jaw dropped. "What?!"

"Yeah, crazy, huh?"

"You're adopted?"

"Not really."

"You lost me."

"Long story short...I was switched at birth."

"No way!" His eyes widened.

"There's more."

"Go on," he said skeptically.

"I met my biological father over spring break and then he was killed." Tears formed in my eyes.

"Seriously? I can't believe you've been going through this alone. I wish you had talked to me."

"I know. I'm sorry."

"Is she fighting for custody?"

"No. She just wants to get to know me."

"Wow." He ran his hand through his hair. "Are you okay?"

I nodded. "It's been a really wild year. I'm ready for the surprises to be over. I just want to move on."

He put his hand on mine. "Then let's do that. Let's move on."

I nodded and dabbed my eyes. Leaning over, I rested my head on his shoulder for a few minutes. A peaceful feeling swept over me. Even though I couldn't tell Adam everything, I had gotten a lot off my chest.

Afterwards, Adam drove me home and walked me to the door. I faced him and said, "Thanks."

"For what?"

"Being you." I leaned in and kissed him. My body warmed at his touch, but it didn't tingle and feel alive like it did when I kissed Kallan. I pushed that thought from my mind and focused on Adam. I ran my hand up his neck and placed it on the back of his head. The kiss grew more intense until finally we broke apart. "See you later," I said and walked inside my house.

I called out for my parents, relieved when nobody answered. I could use the alone time.

When I was sure I was alone, I dropped my glamour. Even though I always saw myself as a faery, it felt like I was lying to the world when I had glamour on, which was ironic since faeries couldn't lie. I stretched my wings and flapped them a few times. I missed the way Kallan would touch them, even if it had only been a couple of times. There was something about his touch.

"Stop it, Rylie," I chastised myself. Thinking of Kallan would only bring back bad memories. I had to put him out of my mind. I was free now. This was what I wanted.

I managed an hour's worth of homework, and my parents still hadn't gotten home from work. I glanced at the time—not quite four. I tried Sierra again.

She finally answered. "What?"

"Really? This is how it's gonna be?" I snapped.

"I don't know what to say to you right now, Ry. I'm pissed."

"Why? Because I want out of that life?"

"Well...yeah. You had it so good. Why throw it away? And you said some really mean things to me."

Had it good? Was she kidding? "Ever since I found out I was a faery, my life has been a mess. I just want to go back to normal and that means I lose our friendship?"

She was silent for a minute. "You're not losing me. I'm just mad at you right now."

I sighed. "What's that supposed to mean?"

"I want your life, Ry. I'm jealous. And I think you're stupid to throw it away."

"Glad to know what you think of me." I pulled the phone away and my finger hovered over the 'End' button, but Sierra's voice pulled me back.

"Ry...I don't mean it that way."

I hated fighting with Sierra. I could only remember fighting with her two times. Sure, we had little spats, but nothing that lasted more than a minute or two. This time seemed like a bigger deal, and I wondered if we'd be able to make up.

We listened to each other breathe for a minute, tension hanging on the line between us. I caved first. "I'm sorry I said the things I did. I was upset."

She didn't answer.

I sighed. "How long are you gonna be mad at me?"

"I don't know." She took a shaky breath. "Drake won't see me right now because of all this."

"What are you talking about?"

"He seems to think he can't get involved with humans right now. It sucks, Rylie. I feel so much for him. I'm alive when he's near. This is something I've never felt before..."

She was describing the way I felt when around Kallan.

"I want to be with him," she finished

I shrugged, even though she couldn't see me. "Then be with him."

"How?"

"I have no idea, Sierra," I said bitterly. "I'm just sick of being told who I can and can't be with. You shouldn't have to deal with that either."

Sierra took a breath that echoed in the line. "I'm sorry. I haven't been there for you since..."

My lip quivered. I bit it to keep from crying. "I'm

sorry, too. I've been a bitch to you. I just don't know what to do. I don't want to fight anymore."

"You've been through a lot."

"I have. And it hurts not being able to lean on my best friend. We've always been there for each other. I need you right now."

I tried not to cry in the mouthpiece, but I wasn't very good at hiding it.

"Feel better?" Sierra asked when I'd finally managed to get some control over my emotions.

"I needed that."

"Ry, is there more to this than just Oren dying?"

I pulled my pillow tight against my stomach and crossed my legs. "Yeah."

"The promise is broken..."

"I think I'm in love with Kallan," I whispered.

"And Adam?"

"I love him, too." I fiddled with my fingers, tears filling my eyes again. "Kallan's dad killed Oren. How do I get over that? How do I love someone whose father is a monster? What if he turns into one, too?"

"You're a good judge of character, Rylie. Do you think Kallan could be like that?"

I thought about Kallan for a minute. "No. He acts tough, but inside he's a good guy."

"Maybe you should trust your instincts."

"What about the fact that he didn't stop them?" I asked.

"Do you think he would have been able to?"

"I don't know. He could have tried." Honestly, with Varwik's immunity, he probably couldn't have. But he didn't try to do anything, not until I got hurt.

"What if he had done something and gotten killed?"

Why did she have to have such good points? "I'm

not sure I can forgive him yet."

"Why does he need to be forgiven?"

"I don't know! I just feel like part of it is his fault. Ugh!" I put my head in my hand, holding the phone tight to my ear.

"Have you talked to Azura since...since your dad was killed?"

"No." I sighed. "Sierra, I don't want anything to do with that world anymore. I want to be human. I want to do normal mundane things."

"You're not human though, Ry. God, that's weird to say. You're a faery. You belong in that world. Or at least to be a part of it. I know none of this is easy, but it's your fate."

"My fate..." I shook my head.

"You need to talk to your parents, Azura, and maybe Kallan. Find out how you feel."

I knew she was right. "How did you get so wise?"

Sierra laughed. "I don't know. Now can we talk about me?"

"You? Sure. What do you want?"

"Drake."

"What can I do?"

"I have to be with him, Ry."

"Then we'll find you a way."

She giggled. "All right."

I still wasn't sure what I could do, but I'd try.

CHAPTER TWENTY-NINE

I didn't waste any time after I got off the phone with Sierra.

I'd made things right with my best friend—well, as right as they could be right now on the heels of a really bad fight. So now I needed to speak with Azura and let her know how I felt. I owed her that.

I was determined to be strong and stand my ground. If she could respect that I wanted to stay in the human world for now, then maybe I could see her every once in a while. I called and left a message on her cell phone. The next time she had service, she'd get my message. Could be minutes, hours, or days.

My parents still weren't home from work by the time Azura knocked softly on the front door. I was bent over my extra credit for math class, slowly working my way through each equation and double-checking my answers.

My heart fluttered as I rushed downstairs and threw open the door.

"It's good to see you," Azura said. When she held out her arms, I walked right into them. And for the first time, it felt good.

I pushed that thought aside and spoke against her shoulder. "Thank you for giving me some space."

"Of course, my love." She gripped me by the shoulders and held me away, running a critical eye over me. "I'm sorry you had to see your father die."

I nodded, glad she had been filled in on what happened and I didn't have to do it. "It was hard."

"I'm sure it was." She brushed my hair from my face, her gaze softening. "You don't have to talk about it."

I didn't respond, but led her to the kitchen and offered her a glass of iced tea. She declined. I poured myself a glass and took a seat across from her. I could see in her eyes that she was wondering why I'd called her here if it wasn't to talk about what had happened.

No tiptoeing around the subject, I told myself. Just do it. "I want to stay here, live here, be as human as I can be."

Azura's face fell. "Oh. I'm sorry to hear that."

I felt guilty. "It's not you. In fact, I was hoping that we could continue spending time together...just here."

"I understand. You have not had a good experience with our world."

That was an understatement. The faery world was beautiful and mysterious. I loved being there, especially in the light faery lands. It would be easy to just go there and forget the human world. But that's not what I wanted.

"You're free now," Azura reminded me. "You don't have to marry Kallan. You could just come home with me and marry whoever you choose."

I could hear the desperation in her voice. "What if that is Adam? Could I live in your world and still marry him?"

"I'm sure we could work it out."

"We could?" Her words shocked me. I didn't think I'd be allowed to be with Adam at all. Now she was saying it was possible? Maybe she was just telling me what I wanted to hear.

"There would be lots to discuss."

I could tell she wasn't telling me everything, and I wasn't sure I wanted to push it before I even had time to think about it. "It's more than that though. I want to go to college, have a career, that stuff."

"Oleander..." Azura clasped her hands on the tabletop and stared down at them. "I'm not sure you understand how important you are to our world. You're an..."

"Aurorian. I know."

"You are meant to do so much in your life."

"That's what you keep telling me."

"It's true."

I knew it was because faeries couldn't lie. I didn't want to hurt Azura. I really didn't. But she wasn't hearing me. She had such high hopes and here I was crushing them. "I'm sorry. Maybe I'll feel differently later on."

"Is it Kallan?" Azura asked. "Is he the reason you don't wish to come back?"

"Partly."

"You're in love with him."

"Yes." I closed my eyes. I hated the honesty thing sometimes. "But I love Adam, too."

"I know. I'm sorry this is hard for you."

"I have another year left of school. I don't plan on

going anywhere until then. Not for Adam, Kallan, or you. I want to finish school."

"I want you to finish school, too." She stood, and we hugged. "I will always support you, Rylie."

It wasn't until after she'd left that I realized she'd finally called me "'Rylie."

Back in my bedroom, I picked up my phone and groaned. Adam had texted me a bunch of times.

Ry we need to talk.

U ok?

Wanna do something?

How's 5 sound?

I looked at the time. My heart sunk when I realized it was past five. I quickly texted him back. *Sorry. Family issues.*

The phone buzzed seconds later. *Talk 2 me*

I didn't know how to reply, so I just shoved the phone back in my pocket.

I tagged along that evening as my mom went shopping for dinner. While she was ordering chicken in the deli, I wandered aimlessly around the CDs and movies, and eventually found myself standing in front of a shelf with a bunch of Rubik's Cubes on it.

The conversation between Kallan and me came back. That day felt so long ago. I picked one up and headed to the register. I wasn't sure what I was going to do with it. It reminded me of Kallan, and for some unknown reason, I wanted him to have it.

I decided to put it on a tree stump just past the tree line. I placed a piece of paper with Kallan's name on it underneath the cube. If he came back, he'd find it.

While Mom and Dad were making dinner, I swung

on the front porch, my thoughts in turmoil after the two emotional conversations. Being outside in the warm weather helped clear my head.

I thought again about everything that had happened. Seemed like I couldn't wrap my mind around it enough to form any conclusions. My heart still felt like it was torn in two, and my phone burned in my pocket, reminding me I still hadn't texted Adam back.

A shadow fell before me. I looked up.

Kallan.

I leapt to my feet. Seeing his face made all the old thoughts that I was trying to work through come flooding back, and I let my emotions get the best of me.

"Why didn't you do something?" I asked him, pounding on his chest.

He didn't skip a beat. "What was I supposed to do?"

"Stop your father? Stop mine? Something. Anything."

"I stopped you, Rylie."

"Me?"

"You accessed dark magick. I used my power to stop you before you did something you would regret."

"What are you saying, Kallan?"

"Didn't you feel different?" Kallan's eyes searched mine.

I nodded, remembering the rush of power. I took his hand and led him down the porch steps and away from the house. I didn't want my parents overhearing our conversation. "Kallan, I don't know what happened out there." I looked down at my feet, unable to meet his eyes. "I felt—strange, powerful for once, and then nothing."

"You tried to stop the fight using my father's ability to access dark magick. It would have worked, but you wouldn't have been able to live with yourself. There is always a price when you use dark magick," he explained.

"You're saying I could have saved my father and you stopped me?" My whole body tensed up.

"You would have taken life from the trees and animals that surrounded the area. The price was too great."

"I still don't understand." I took a few steps away from him further into the yard.

He followed me. "Your power is very dangerous in the wrong hands. If you had accessed dark magick, not only would you have taken the life energy from others, you would have lost any chance of bridging the gap between the light and dark worlds. I told you I would never use my power on you, but I couldn't allow you to do something you would regret. You don't even understand the consequences. It was not our fight, Rylie. It was between our fathers."

"I would have killed things? I didn't even know I was doing it! Why didn't your father use dark magick to kill Oren?"

"Ego. I doubt he thought Oren had the slightest chance of killing him."

I could see that. Varwik was the definition of arrogance.

"You need to learn to control your power and how to use it for good. Rylie, you need to spend more time in our realm where you belong."

"I can't think about that right now."

"I understand, but you can't run away from your responsibility forever." Kallan reached into his pocket and pulled out the Rubik's Cube, tossing it up in the air with one hand and catching it with the other. "Got your present," he said.

I was relieved he let the subject drop for now. He always knew how to read me and knew when to back off. "I see that."

"What do I do with it?"

"You mix it up and then return it so that each side is only one color."

He studied it. "Interesting."

"You said you liked puzzles."

"I do." He gave me his beautiful grin. "I thought you were mad at me."

"Then why did you come tonight?" I asked.

"I wanted to see you. I miss you. Plus I wanted to find out what the gift meant." He shook the Rubik's Cube.

I wanted to return his smile, but I couldn't. "I'm not mad. I'm...confused."

"You just have to listen to your heart."

"Easy for you to say."

He scoffed. "I was closed off and unemotional until you. Ever since I laid eyes on you...since you came into my life...all I've wanted to do is be with you. I want to love you and for you to love me. I'm not confused. I know exactly what I want."

There was such conviction in his voice that I was stunned by his words. I knew he loved me, but I hadn't known how much. I stood there like an idiot, speechless. I couldn't move, I couldn't speak. I knew if I opened my mouth, I'd admit to him that I loved him. And I still had my life here in the human realm. How could I just run off with him because I loved him? It wouldn't be fair to anyone.

When I finally spoke, the words came out soft. "I need some time to think."

"That's what you always say. You never come

back with an answer. Finish this chapter, so you can move on to the next."

It wasn't just a chapter, it was a whole book. "I..."

Kallan put his finger to my lips. "I will always give you what you want...time, space, anything. I will wait for you." He took a step closer. "I've tried hard to stay away."

"Obviously." I could feel the warmth of his body so close to mine. My heart pattered somewhere in my stomach.

"I don't want to hurt you."

"Our fathers are dead. The promise is broken. We're both free. Can't you just move on?"

He moved closer again. Reaching out, he pushed back a strand of hair that had fallen in my face. "I don't want to, and I don't think you do either."

"You're a dark faery and I'm a light faery. The worlds are too different." Even to my own ears, it felt like I was making excuses.

"What if they didn't have to be? Things are different now. We could bring peace to our lands together." Kallan stared at me in the twilight. His brows knitted together. "What else is wrong, Rylie?"

It didn't surprise me that Kallan could read me so well. Our connection went beyond anything I could understand.

I took a shaky breath. "It's just...I've known him over ten years. We've been together for three. We were supposed to go to college, get married, have kids, and now... Now it's all falling apart."

"Maybe it's not falling apart, maybe it's all coming together."

I had loved Adam for years. I still did. He was safe. Normal. Familiar. Human. But I was in love with Kallan too. Unfamiliar. Different. Exciting. How could

I love two boys at the same time? No matter what I did, one of them would get hurt.

"Kallan..." My voice trailed off. I didn't know whether to ask him to leave or ask him to kiss me.

Before I could say anything, Kallan closed the space between us and wrapped me in his arms. It felt so right, so perfect... I forgot the fight with Sierra and the pain in Azura's eyes as I broke her heart. I just let Kallan hold me.

"Rylie?"

I leapt away from Kallan as if there were fire between us.

I gasped. "Adam!"

CHAPTER THIRTY

"What the hell is going on here?!" Adam's voice boomed. My heart dropped to my toes, and I quickly took a few steps back. How long had he been there?

His eyes were narrowed and his face an unhealthy shade of red.

I looked from Kallan to Adam. "It's not what you think." Ugh! How lame did that sound?

Adam was already stalking over to us, fists clenched at his sides. "Who do you think you are? Coming to our school, trying to take my position in baseball, and now moving in on my girl?"

Kallan pushed me behind him and faced Adam. "Calm down."

"You ass..." Adam threw a punch, hitting Kallan square in the jaw.

Kallan rubbed his jaw. "You really don't want to do this."

"Like hell I don't!" Adam threw another punch.

Reacting from the blow, Kallan shook his head and drew back his fist.

"Stop it!" I screamed.

Their fists froze in midair. "Stay out of this, Rylie," Adam snarled.

"No. This isn't Kallan's fault. It's mine. If you want to hit someone, hit me."

"I'm not going to hit you, Rylie." Adam pulled back and looked up at me like he was seeing me for the first time. Shame washed over his face.

"Then put your hands down." I turned towards Kallan. "You too."

They both dropped their hands to their sides and stood up, stepping a few feet away from each other. Adam's intense eyes gave me a once-over. "Is this why you've been so distant lately? You found yourself a new boyfriend? I should have known." He shook his head in disgust.

"It's not that, but we need to talk. Alone."

I walked over towards Kallan. I pulled him over to the side and whispered, "I need you to leave. This is between me and Adam. Please just go."

"Do you want me to tell him to forget what he saw here? He won't remember what happened. You could go back to normal." His whole body tensed. I knew it was hard for him to say.

A selfless act.

"You'd do that for me?"

"I'd do anything for you."

A small smile crept upon my face. "No. Adam and I need to have this talk. It's been coming for a while now."

"Okay." He turned and walked away towards the street so Adam didn't see him disappear into the woods. I took a deep breath and hoped I had the strength to do what was right.

"Let's go inside." I brushed past Adam and crossed the lawn, making my way into the house. He followed close behind, but didn't say a word. I sat at the table and clasped my hands in my lap to try and stop the shaking. I looked into Adam's beautiful green eyes and opened my mouth, but the words wouldn't come.

When I didn't start talking, he did. "Something has been going on the last few months, Rylie. I don't know what it is. I feel like we've lost our connection. You didn't tell me what you were going through for a long time. We used to tell each other everything."

"I know. I'm so sorry, Adam. I never meant for any of this to happen."

"Are you and that guy together?" he asked. I could hear the disdain in his voice.

"No." It wasn't a lie; technically we weren't together. "I guess I've changed. Things in my life have changed. I never meant to hurt you." I wiped away the tears that were falling down my cheeks.

"So are we breaking up? Is that what you're trying to tell me?"

His question was a simple one and yet it was one I didn't want to answer. I knew this was coming, but I still felt crushed. The air left me and I started shaking. Sobs soon took over my body. I had been with Adam for as long as I could remember. I felt mad that we were calling it quits after a rocky few months, but somewhere deep down inside me, I knew it was right.

"Yes. I'm sorry."

His eyes were wet and he looked out the window to avoid looking at me. "I never imagined you and I would break up."

"Me either."

I reached out for his hand, but he yanked it away.

"I'm gonna go."

"I'm so sorry, Adam. I..."

"Don't." He stood up and slipped out the door.

My heart broke as his truck pulled away. I watched until it was gone out of sight, and then I ran up to my room, passing my mom on the way. I threw myself on my bed and cried, my heart open and exposed.

Rain began to fall against the window, mimicking my tears.

There were so many things left unspoken, but I knew then I was holding on to a dream that wasn't going to come true. A future that I couldn't have. It was time to let it all go. Even though I knew I made the right choice it didn't make it any easier.

CHAPTER
THIRTY-ONE

After a while, there was a knock on my door. When I didn't answer, the door swung open and Sierra walked in. She gave me a sympathetic look and sat down next to me on the bed.

"Why are you here?" I asked.

"Your mom called. She said she thought I should come." She opened her arms and I leaned into them. "What happened?"

As I filled her in on the break-up, I started sobbing again.

She rubbed my back and murmured, "It's going to be okay."

I played with my bracelet and wondered aloud, "What's going to happen now?"

"I don't know, but for what it's worth, I think breaking up with Adam was the right thing. I love Adam, you know that, but when I see the way you look at Kallan...it's different. I don't know if that's what you want to hear right now, but that's what I see." She stroked my hair and tucked it behind my ear.

"I broke Adam's heart," I told her.

"I know," she said with a sigh.

I felt numb as we sat in silence for a while longer. "I don't know what to do now. Every dream I ever had is gone."

"Maybe it's time to dream of a new future," Sierra suggested. "Dig deep into your heart."

I closed my eyes. Maybe Kallan and Sierra were right. Maybe it was a sign. Maybe my life was coming together instead of falling apart. Fate. I needed to take a chance. I always chose the comfortable route. My heart knew what it wanted—something different and exciting. Kallan?

The door opened and Mom walked in with two bowls of ice cream. "Thought you girls could use some."

I sat up straight and took one of the bowls. "Thanks, Mom. You're the best."

She grinned and kissed my forehead, and said, "I love you," before slipping out of the room.

Wanting to change the subject, I asked Sierra about her life. "Seen Drake recently?"

"We were together earlier." Her eyes turned all dreamy. "He's the best thing that's ever happened to me."

"Gee, thanks," I joked.

She rolled her eyes. "Guy-wise, Rylie. You'll always be my best friend."

"Even if I'm not always here."

"Yes. No matter where you are." She shoved a spoonful of ice cream in her mouth. "Do you think I'll be able to be with Drake?"

"I said we'd find a way. I keep my promises." I finished my ice cream. "Let's go to the faery realm."

"Really?" Sierra's face lit up.

"Yeah...I want to talk to my aunt." I had an idea—one that meant I'd have to go into the faery realm sooner than I had wanted.

Sierra spent the night at my house. In the morning, after eating one of the special foods I asked Nessa to drop off, we headed for the trees. The sky was dark and overcast. It was definitely springtime with all the rain we were getting. I found Azura's with ease. Every time I came it got easier. But I wasn't bound for my faery mother's tree house. After leaving Sierra with Drake and promising to meet up with her later, I made a hard right and mounted the gnarled wooden steps at Lorella's.

She swung it open. "Oleander. I was expecting you."

Not surprising. "I need a favor."

"Please, come in." She stepped aside and held the door open.

I passed by her into her living room. "I was hoping you could take a peek at my future again."

"I can if you'd like, but I'm not sure I'll have answers for you."

I nodded. "It would really help me if I knew a little more about what's in store for me."

"Let's sit." She sat in one of two armchairs that faced each other, so I sat in the other.

Taking my hands in hers, Lorella closed her eyes and took deep breaths. "The darkness is gone. Your future is bright. It will be filled with adventure. You have come to a crossroads...you were forced to make a decision." She opened her eyes.

"Did I decide right?" I wasn't positive I really wanted to know the answer.

"Shhh." Her lips curled up and she opened her eyes. "Do you remember when I told you sometimes we don't need to know and we should just let things unfold?"

"Yes."

"This is one of those times. You will find love and happiness. You will have a life some only dream of. But you do not need to know everything your life has in store for you."

"So you can't or won't tell me what to do from here?"

"No. I know you want me to, but I think it's more important for you to find your way."

A thought flew across my mind. I still had her hands. I wondered if I could see my own future. "What about my parents?" I asked, trying to distract her. "Will they be okay?"

She closed her eyes again, and I did the same. I concentrated on my breathing and tried to imagine the future. I tried to picture my wedding day. And suddenly images came to my mind...but they weren't of me. Lorella was at a wedding; not mine, but Violet's. What was going on?

Lorella yanked her hands from mine, and I snapped my eyes open. "You're sneaky," she said wryly. "Using your power to get to mine."

I looked down, ashamed. "I'm sorry. I'm just at a loss. Everything has fallen apart."

"Rest assured, Oleander, you will be fine. Your parents, too."

"Why didn't I see my future?"

"I can't see my own, only others'. What did you see?"

I smiled. "Yours. You were at Violet's wedding."

Her eyes widened. "Really? Who does she marry?"

I laughed. "Wouldn't you like to know?" Truth was, I didn't know myself. I only saw the back of the midnight-blue-winged faery and didn't know who he was. "Sometimes we don't need to know."

She looked shocked at first, but then she smiled. "You're learning."

I nodded and stood up. "I should be going."

Lorella walked me to the door and opened it. "It was nice to see you. You should visit more often."

"I'll try." I didn't want to promise, but I had a feeling that despite my earlier decision to stay away, I'd be visiting the faery realm more often.

It was getting closer to the end of the school year. We were studying for our end-of-course exams. I hated every minute of it, but I studied hard, hoping that I'd get good grades.

Kallan never showed his face in school again. He kept his promise—no surprise there. He gave me plenty of time and space. My eyes constantly searched the tree line for a glimpse of him. Each day my heart fell when he wasn't there, but I didn't let it keep me down.

One afternoon in late May, Drake was waiting for us to get home from school so he could hang out with Sierra. This was becoming an everyday thing for them. I got out of the car, intent on getting a snack before studying for my last exam, when Drake approached me. "I've got some interesting news."

"Oh?" My eyebrows rose.

"Kallan moved out of the castle and into some little cottage…"

My mind wandered back to the cottage he showed me, the one where he painted. It would make a much better home for him than that cold castle would.

"...apparently he's been painting a lot too. Oh, and he let all the servants go. Told them to go back to their families. Paid them very well. Not only that, but he's invited any of us to go into the dark realm and use any resources we want," Drake rambled.

"Wow. Have you seen him?"

"No." He studied me. "Maybe you should talk to him?"

I nodded and muttered a "thank you" before going inside and eating a snack. Focusing on schoolwork was too hard now that my mind was thinking about Kallan. Would Kallan really try to make a difference in the faery realms even if I wasn't there? Would he be successful?

I couldn't believe he had moved out of the castle. I had never liked that place. I knew it would never feel like home. I was glad that Kallan was out of there and somewhere cozier.

I lay in my bed thinking until my eyes closed...

I was standing in a field in the faery realm wearing a long pink dress. I could hear piskies playing in the woods nearby. It was a beautiful day, warm and sunny. Kallan stood at my side and pulled me close to him. He held my face in his hands. My wings were fluttering like crazy as he leaned in and kissed me.

"Look around," he said, stretching out his arm to show me miles and miles of beautiful faery land. Rolling hills, fields of flowers, magnificent creatures. "This can all be ours."

"How?" I whispered.

"You just have to choose it. Come and do what you were born to do."

A loud clap of thunder startled me awake. I must have fallen asleep. What a crazy dream! I ran my hand through my hair. I needed some air. I walked downstairs and onto the back porch, watching as the lighting from the thunderstorm lit up the night sky. Call me crazy, but I enjoyed a good storm.

A flash of lightning in the distance revealed Kallan standing in the yard. My heart skipped a beat and my wings fluttered behind me. Fate. Suddenly I knew. I couldn't explain it. I just knew. I belonged with him.

I hurried down the porch steps and ran to him. We stood toe-to-toe with the rain splashing at our feet. My hair was pasted against my face.

Standing there face-to-face with Kallan, I couldn't deny my feelings anymore. I grabbed Kallan, pulled him close to me, and touched my wet lips to his. The slow kiss was soon replaced with a more passionate one and my body exploded into fireworks. I pulled away to catch my breath, but kept our foreheads touching. I looked into Kallan's eyes, our hands entwining between us. He smiled, and my heart soared.

This was me. All me.

No promises.

About the Authors:

Talia Jager

When Talia isn't hiding in the bathroom from her six children, munching on a chocolate bar, she enjoys hiking the red rocks in Utah or sitting on the beach with a Kindle in her hands and her toes in the ocean.

Talia has written a number of books for young adults, including *Damaged: Natalie's Story, Teagan's Story: Her Battle With Epilepsy, If I Die Young, Secret Bloodline, Lost and Found,* and *The Gifted Teens Series.* Connect with Talia online at *www.taliajager.com* or by email at *taliajager@att.net*

Links:
www.taliajager.com
taliajager.blogspot.com
www.facebook.com/taliajager
www.facebook.com/authortaliajager
www.twitter.com/taliajager
amazon.com/author/taliajager

Julia Crane

Julia Crane is the author of the YA paranormal fiction novels: Keegan's Chronicles, Freak of Nature, Mesmerized and Eternal Youth. Julia has believed in magical creatures since the day her grandmother first told her an Irish tale. She has traveled far and wide to all the places her grandmother told her about, gaining inspiration from her journeys to places like Nepal, Cyprus, Sri Lanka, Italy, France and many more. And who knows? Maybe the magical creatures she writes about are people she met along the way.

Julia Crane has a bachelor's degree in criminal justice. Although she's spent most of her life on the US east coast, she currently lives in Dubai with her husband and three children.

Links:
www.juliacrane.com
www.amazon.com/Julia-Crane/e/B0055HYSHY
www.twitter.com/juliacrane2
juliacrane@zoho.com

30813095R00159

Made in the USA
Lexington, KY
21 March 2014